Clearwater

A BOLDENE ROMANCE

ESTHER STAR

CLEARWATER

A BOLDENE ROMANCE (BOOK 1)

ESTHER STAR

SWALLOWTAIL INK

∿

Get new release updates and exclusive content when you sign up for my
newsletter at www.estherstar.com!

DEDICATION

For my darling, Sophie.
You came along and filled me
with so much to say.

ACKNOWLEDGMENTS

Thank you to Robert, my impeccable soulmate, for seeing me and freeing my wings. You have eliminated any excuse I might have had for not taking this leap. How can I ever return the favor?

Thank you to my beautiful modern family and long-time friends; Stef and Soli, your support is my creative sustenance. A special thank you to Amy. We spent countless hours at our machines together, and you kept me in stitches—may Mnemosyne Designs live forever! (Hint to my readers: search Etsy.)

Last, but not least, thank you to Paolo (you are irreplaceable to me), Caroline, Flic, Lucia, and Aaron: my divine companions on this celestial adventure.

1

*N*o one can drive or ride a bike down main street in Boldene. It's been a pedestrian mall for nearly fifty years. Simone Bonhomme kicks her leg across the bar on her bike and coasts on one pedal anyway, weaving through the people walking on their way to local jobs. In the morning before work everyone is in a hurry, and Simone can tell they are annoyed at the way she bends the rules and rides her bike where she shouldn't. She knows it's rude, and she sees the people staring her down every morning. She smiles in defense, but internally curses the cobblestone and the reverberations it sends up her spine, the long night she spent sewing, and the kink in her neck.

As Simone locks up her bike, her phone chimes. A quick glance tells her it is a message about her biggest and most demanding private client, Ballistic Bride. Resisting the urge to cringe, Simone makes a mental note to read it when she has a moment. Near the coffee stand, she finds one of her best friends, Aurora.

Aurora Copper sits at a tiny table under the kiosk's awning

perched on a folding chair. Dressed in all black, she wears dark sunglasses and a leather jacket.

Aurora interrupts the photo she is taking of her coffee to say, "I thought you were going to stand me up for the first time in ten years."

"Sorry I'm so late. I still have about fifteen minutes, do you?"

Aurora looks at the time. "Just that much."

Simone gets a cup of coffee and a scone and sits back down.

"Forget to shower this morning?"

Simone scalds her tongue on black coffee. "That was so harsh! Yes, I might have, but you are as guilty of it as I am. You just fake it with your uniform. Wearing the same thing every day. No makeup, red lips. Platinum hair so short you don't have to brush it. Or wash it. Why does it look better dirty?"

Aurora brushes invisible crumbs off her lapel. "I know you're just jealous because I've got that part of life hacked." She smiles and takes a chunk of Simone's scone.

Simone reaches for a bite of Aurora's croissant. "Uniforms confine me." She takes a big bite, hoping the pastries will keep her stomach occupied until quitting time at five. Lunch out is a luxury she saves for Sundays. The money Simone has left in her bank account needs to last long enough for the stack of bills on her fridge to eat it alive by month's end.

"This isn't a uniform. This is a lifestyle choice. Besides, you are distracting me from my point. The only time you show up unkempt for anything is when you've worked until just before daylight and then slept through the alarm."

"That demon. He terrorizes me with his angry red eyes." Simone cringes thinking about how she had to tear herself away from the blissful cocoon of soft sheets. "Anyway, please, don't chastise me for working too much and keeping late hours. You do it, too."

Aurora shrugs. "I know. But I work for myself. You work for James Ficklow and everyone knows--"

"Ficklow's a dick." Everyone of Simone's friends agrees with her on that.

Aurora takes a peek at her phone and it gives Simone reprieve. She chuckles. Something she's reading makes her blush. Aurora looks different this morning. Something about her is off. She is smiling under her scowl.

"Spill it, Dawn Star, what's up with you?" Simone can only wonder.

Aurora pushes her sunglasses up, hiding the brilliant green of her eyes. She schools her expression. "What? Nothing."

"Right. Spill it. Where have you been?" Simone says this like she's talking to a puppy whose just been raiding the pantry.

Aurora rolls her eyes. It is like pulling teeth to get her to open up. Simone has to ask a lot of questions to get a complete view of what it felt like. Aurora answers every single one, reluctantly. Ever since early on in college, Aurora has made good money photographing weddings, and some of Simone's first clients have wound up being Aurora's as well, and vis-à-vis. Turns out she was photographing a wedding in Big Sur.

"I bet it was beautiful," Simone prompts.

"It was. All girly and glowing. As a designer you would have loved her dress."

"What did you do to balance out all that gooey sweetness?"

"I had hot sex with a near stranger, then picked up a dangerous private eye assignment."

Simone chokes on her last bite of scone. Her coffee is gone. She reaches for Aurora's cup and regrets it. There is cream in her coffee, and Simone finds that disgusting. "Yuck."

"It was good sex, actually. No yuck factor at all."

Simone giggles. "I yucked over the cream, not the sex, and not the PI work, either. Although we will talk about how you said you were done with that later. Who is the stranger?"

3

And this is where Simone can see Aurora start to squirm. Aurora never lies. It's a core principle she holds above all others. But Aurora also doesn't like to bare her soul, especially not in public over coffee before nine in the morning. Simone does her best not to press, but Aurora said 'near' and it makes her wonder. She picks at the crumbs on her napkin. "Is your stranger anyone I know?"

Aurora shrugs and looks away.

Simone waits.

After a minute or two, Aurora turns directly to Simone. "You are exhausted and overworked."

It is Simone's turn to squirm. Whenever Aurora turns the conversation back on her, Simone knows Aurora is done talking about whatever. Ironically, this is one of the things Simone appreciates most about her friend. Aurora has strong boundaries and keeps her private life very private. Asking about others is her version of a graceful exit. "You are right, I'm tired."

"How are things with your label?"

"Good. Really good. I've wrapped up a bridal gown and three bridesmaids dresses this past weekend so I can focus on finishing the rest of Ballistic Bride's order."

Aurora's eyebrows lift at the mention of Simone's most difficult client. "I thought that order shipped early last week."

"It did, but then she decided to add two more bridesmaids' dresses. I should be able to squeak them in before I need to get started on other orders due later next month. That reminds me, give me a second, an email just came in from her." Simone scans her phone.

"Isn't her wedding in a few weeks?"

"Just a little over three weeks. If the photos are as good as yours, I'll have a really nice spread for my portfolio and the main page on my website. A bride plus her twelve maids makes a baker's dozen..."

Simone's voice falls off as she reads. She sucks in a breath and covers her mouth. "Oh no...no. But...No...I'm not doing this. It's too much. There isn't time." She turns white and passes her phone to Aurora.

Aurora reads the message and bursts into laughter. "How rich."

"She wants custom garters for herself and the bridal party," Simone continues. "Then three hundred sixty-five garters—one for every woman she is inviting to the wedding. One for every day of wedded bliss in the year. That's three hundred and seventy-eight garters."

"Wait," Aurora pauses. "She doesn't mean the embroidered garters, does she?"

Simone's eyes widen. "Yes, keep reading."

"Easy, Bambi," Aurora cautions Simone and reads out loud, "Guest garters...in gray satin, embroidered with guest's names. List to follow."

"What am I—" Simone looks to her friend with dismay on her face. "Why?"

Aurora cocks her head in reply and says, "Why not? This bride's a gem. I bet she gets everything she asks her daddy for. Imagine the inevitable nightmare with guest names and last minute RSVPs. Is it worth it?"

"She's my biggest and best order to date. Things have turned out beautifully. I have a signed agreement from both her and her photographer to use the images for my marketing. I need this order to be perfect." Simone can't fathom how she is going to sew that many silly garters and stay on top of her other work. She adjusts things around in her mind, rearranging her schedule to find time.

Aurora interrupts her. "Hire help."

Simone physically balks at the idea.

Aurora keeps at it. "Hire someone to just sew the garters. Whomever it is never even has to touch the dresses. I know you are all particular about that. You want to sew every stitch on every piece to leave your studio, but there comes a time when you have to level up and delegate. Share the wealth."

Simone narrows her eyes at Aurora. "You had to say that word, didn't you?"

"What? Share? Does the only child in you shrink at the idea?" Simone's eyes worry in response to her tone, and Aurora softens her delivery a little. "Look, I'm not talking about taking on a partner or someone sharing the credit or doing the design work. I'm talking about someone coming in to help you sew an obscene number of garters. Someone who could free you up to work on more important parts of your business. Time is money, Sim. Are you willing to miss a bigger deadline over garters?"

"I'm responsible. I want a fantastic review and recommendation. This is me and my *Bonhomme* label. My reputation. Ballistic Bride has a huge social media following."

Simone puts her head down on the table, resting it there for a minute. The surface is stone cold, and it staves off her rising sense of panic. "Of course, her wedding is her everything."

In a far off voice Aurora replies, "It's hard to hear you, Sim, with your head in the sand."

Simone picks her head up.

Aurora continues, "Business owners hire employees."

"I barely pay myself."

"How many hours do you think you have given Ficklow this week?"

"What day is today?"

"Very funny."

"Two too many hours." Simone startles herself when she checks the time. "Craptastic." She gathers her trash and kisses Aurora on the cheek. "Laters, I'm late."

"Spaters, gater. Ficklow is a dick, remember that."

Aurora's reply echoes in Simone's ears as she runs across the mall to Ficklow Fashion.

~

Simone opens the front door just enough to sneak inside but not enough to trigger the bell. Almost as composed as the black and white scene on display in the front window, she smooths her gray dress and enters the back of the store.

Before she can sneak past his office door, she sees James Ficklow standing at the threshold.

Simone barely breathes as she walks past.

"Morning," she says.

James is barely taller than Simone at five foot three. Nearly eye to eye it is hard to miss the expression on his face. Simone can tell by the set of his mouth James isn't pleased with her.

He combs his micro beard and evaluates her, starting with her windblown hair. "What we do here works, Simone."

She runs her fingers through her brunette bob, uncomfortable with his hint of disapproval. She can't help but take the tiniest step back when his pasty hand reaches out to arrange the collar of her dress.

Simone knows she has been pushing the line lately, wearing flats and flowy dresses, slipping from his branding, which is much more sober, classic, staid. Given two cocktails, Simone might also call it stale. But she isn't here to reinvent the wheel.

"Everyone on your team has a dress code. White tops, black skirts or trousers. No deviations."

Simone nods her head. She can't help but mentally correct him. There is no team. It's just the two of them now. Last Friday, her only coworker told James he could take his constructive criticism and go fuck himself. Simone sparkles at the memory.

"Perhaps dressing appropriately for work is too much to ask?"

Simone's bristles at his tone of voice. "Of course not." She visualizes the limited black and whites section of her closet.

Flying below the radar is worth the discomfort of heels. "That won't be necessary. I just need to do a pickup at the dry cleaners."

Ficklow mumbles and nods. "How are you on the June Bride launch?"

Simone spent a few extra hours before going home last night to be sure all of the details were ironed out. "Everything is on schedule for production with the designs you've approved. I have the prototypes here, and I'm ready today to pack and ship."

"Before you pack anything, let's take one more look at everything."

Simone cringes. This could take hours, and while her work is really good, nothing is perfect. She laments the loss of her coworker and the distraction of another warm body in the office. Feeling like she is under a spontaneous job review, she reminds herself that at this point, she is all James has for help. Unless he is willing to shoot himself in the foot and miss production deadlines, her job is secure.

But just because a job is secure, doesn't mean it is a good job. Over the next three hours, Simone and James go stitch by stitch through each seam in the summer bridal line. He is ruthless and catches every single thing she wishes she had done better. When James is finally satisfied everything is as good as can be at this point, he gives her permission to pack and ship the order.

Simone works through lunch to be sure the shipment gets out with the day's mail. She's just finished taping and signing for the pickup when James calls her into his office. Simone sucks in a deep breath of relatively fresh air before stepping into the confines of his office. She sits down across from him.

Behind his desk, Ficklow looks pale, almost blue in places, and she wonders why he ties his tie so tight. Immediately after she sits down, he gets up and walks around to the front of the desk. His silk suit barely makes a sound. His cologne is over-whelming.

She pulls slightly back from him.

"I have a new assignment for you," he says, folding his long, skinny fingers together.

Tearing her eyes off the strange map of their crisscrosses, she gets nervous. Something new sounds good. But—her plate is full managing the June Bride distribution and picking up what her coworker abandoned Friday.

Not to mention the bomb Ballistic Bride just dropped.

Still, this isn't her first rodeo. She knows what she is doing. She's been with Ficklow for nearly three years and has the rhythm down. Managing how he dominates her time and the insanely high level of his expectations are the only tricky parts of this job. Creatively, she'll acknowledge it is stifling.

I'm actually suffocating.

Carefully, she replies, "Something new?"

"There is a competition this month. It is a new part of Bold-ene's sister city contract with Berlin. It's called Fashion Bolder." He shrugs. "A play on words, I guess. Anyway, the number of contestants is limited, because there are just a handful of sponsors on our side and it's a trial run. There is a submission process, and competitors will be chosen from among them. It's all very last minute, thrown together and low profile to keep the competition at a minimum while the kinks get ironed out for next year." He walks back behind his desk and sorts through some papers. "It's really for newer designers who need a leg up. Beneath us, all things considered." Offhandedly he drops the other shoe. "The prize is a $50,000 check and a spot in Berlin Fashion Week."

Simone takes a harsh inhale. That kind of prize could launch an emerging label into the next orbit.

James watches her closely. "I want you to put together the

submission for Ficklow Fashion." He hands her a piece of paper with the contest rules and requirements on it.

Simone's head spins. She looks the details over, making a mental list. The contest is on the verge of impossible. One bridal gown and three dresses in three weeks. Submissions are due in one week, contestants are chosen next Friday, and there are three weeks to sew before the show. Which, coincidentally, is the same day as Ballistic Bride's wedding.

Simone asks, "Why don't you draw up the entry?"

James clears his throat and orders the stacks on his already very tidy desk. "Because, like I said, it is practically beneath us to compete at all. I already have the best boutique in Boldene."

Yet Simone knows it's about Berlin. He wants a chance at that. *She* wants a chance at that.

"I'll review your entry first thing next week. And, Simone?" He pauses to be sure he has her full attention.

Simone wants to roll her eyes. "Yes?"

"I'm looking for your best work. Impress me."

2

*S*imone sneaks up behind her good friend, Gemma, and pinches her waist. "Boo."

Gemma's long blonde curls bounce, and her pale mouth breaks into a glossy grin. "Good morning!" Her cat eyes glow a yellow green, and Gemma's upper lids are elegantly lined with black. Gold hoops nest in her ears, and her body flows like the folds of her long dress.

Simone looks down at her skirt and flip-flops and wonders why she doesn't try harder. Gemma Simms likely finished an eight-hour shift at The Salt Lick just hours ago. "How can you walk around in heels all night slinging cocktails and shine like this the next day?"

Gemma pouts just a little bit. "I don't know."

Simone chuckles because this is so Gemma. Clueless about her own charm and effortless beauty.

"What? I'm wearing flip-flops, too?" Gemma pulls up the hem of her dress to reveal sparkly sandals.

"Those don't count." Simone slides her hand through the arm cocked at Gemma's hip and pulls her inside Silver Spoons.

It is Sunday morning, and for as long as she has been

having coffee with Aurora on Fridays, she's been having brunch with Gemma on Sundays at Willow's diner.

As soon as the girls are settled in their booth, Willow Carter emerges from behind her office door. Willow is only a few years older than Gemma and Simone, but she carries herself like she's a decade their senior. A wild mess of copper hair haloes her creamy, heart-shaped face and blue eyes.

On the way to their table, she scoops up a carafe and mugs, then darts around her staff, who weave between customers.

The diner is set up with the soda counter in front of the kitchen, and serves breakfast twenty-four hours a day. It is the nicest place to get both a grease bomb and the hair of the dog.

Willow sits down at their booth and pours them each a cup of thick brew. No one says a word until the first cup is finished and Willow has been interrupted at least three times by regulars.

Finally, Simone relaxes her head against the tall booth and closes her eyes.

Willow interrupts her repose. "You look like shit."

Simone can hear Willow looking at her. She is such a trouble-maker. Even her stare sounds hard. It takes Simone time to reply. "I know, Viking Princess, but anyone would look like shit next to Gemma."

"Enough," Gemma growls. "I put myself together the same way every day."

Simone opens her eyes to glare at Gemma.

Willow angles her head, clearly expecting Simone to say something.

"What? Aurora told me as much already." Simone suddenly feels the truth of what her friends have been telling her. She turns her face to the window and sees her reflection. Her cheeks are sunken and there are dark circles under her eyes. Her bangs are too long, messing with her mascara, and the rest of her shaggy bob is limp, tucked tight behind her ears. She isn't wearing any makeup, not even lip balm. She just rolled out of bed, into the shower, threw some clothes and showed up. "I've been working."

Willow nods her head. "Okay."

Simone hates it when Willow says, *okay*. It means, *and*. "I worked yesterday, late, didn't get much sleep. I chose to sleep in over polishing up this morning." Simone is saying all of the things, the words pouring out of her mouth with unbelievable ease, but she doesn't believe any of her own excuses.

Gemma reaches across the table to touch Simone's hand. "Yesterday was Saturday."

Simone pulls her hand away. "I know. I have a day job and my label, remember?" She doesn't mean to snap at Gemma, it just comes out that way.

"We remember," Willow says. "Were you at home yesterday working on your private orders?"

Simone clenches her jaw. She should have been home working on her orders. Instead, she went into Ficklow's so she could put together their Fashion Bolder submission without James hovering over her every thought and idea. "I should have been. I only meant to go into the store for a couple of hours. We are short staffed, and he gave me another assignment."

"Remind me: you do or don't get paid by the hour?"

Ugh. Willow has to point out the obvious. "You know I don't, but this time the carrot is better than a buck."

She takes a minute or two to describe the contest to Gemma and Willow.

"$50K could go far, and the whole Berlin thing is very excit-ing." Gemma's face is lit up and Simone can tell she is genuinely excited for her.

"I'm just sorry you can't enter it on your own, with your private label," Willow says.

"I know." Simone takes another sip of coffee before contin-uing. "I also went into the office to take another look at my contract on file in my work computer. Entering Fashion Bolder on my own would be a major violation of my contract. The only reason I can still pick up work for my label is because it's work for clients I had before I started at Ficklow, or by word of mouth only. No advertising of any kind. There is a clause in my contract that says I can't do anything else that might be considered to compete with Ficklow Fashion in any way."

Simone spent the better part of yesterday combing through all of the fine print, and considering what a shame it was, and what an opportunity it would be to enter the competition on her own. "The thing is, I'm not sure if I were to enter on my own if my designs would get picked to compete. There is something to be said for having the Ficklow name to submit under. At least I can be sure our entry will get reviewed."

Gemma and Willow glance at each other.

Willow speaks first. "You are more than talented enough to design an entry that would make it through to competition. We all know Ficklow keeps you on because you'll bend over backwards to do a good job there."

"Look, I know I put in way too much time at the day job, but I still believe it is worth it. Wait until you see the June Bride line. I came up with all of the designs, and Ficklow approved sending them to production."

Gemma high fives her over the basket of biscuits that just arrived.

Willow pours another cup of coffee and says, "What about your label? How are orders going there?"

Simone laughs, and it has an edge of mania that scares her a little. She gives her friends the scoop on Ballistic Bride. "She wants to add three hundred and seventy-eight garters, just ad hoc. It's incredible on the one hand, and on the other she strikes me as someone who gets what she wants more often than not." She accepts the honey Willow hands her and drizzles it over the butter Gemma lathered on her biscuit. "Aurora said I should hire help."

Gemma laughs out loud and Willow pats her on the back when she chokes in a particularly unladylike manner. Gemma wipes her eyes and sniffs. "Girl, we have known you for nearly a decade. Was Aurora serious? I'd have voted you least likely to ask for help, and least willing to accept it."

Simone rolls her eyes and admits it. "True. I'm a solopreneur for a reason. I want to be my own boss, make my own decisions, cash the checks and pay myself."

"Sweetness," Willow says gently, "you are handcuffed to that day job. Your status as solopreneur is part-time. How do you feel about that?"

Nauseaus.

The noise in the diner is all at once too much for Simone. Plates and silverware clank together. The smells of hot syrup and crab legs aren't sitting well.

She gets up. "I have to go to the restroom."

She walks as fast as she can to the ladies.' Inside, the smell of air freshener further sickens her, and she locks herself in a stall. Bending over the toilet, she closes her eyes and forces herself to breathe. She is shaking, and a fine sweat breaks out on her forehead and under her eyes. She braces herself with her arms. Her vision starts to close with a shower of stars. She vomits and it sort of makes her feel better. She fights to keep her vision clear and her arms steady so she doesn't make a mess of herself.

The bathroom door opens. Gemma and Willow cluster on the other side of her stall door.

"You alive in there?" Willow asks.

Simone focuses on the toilet handle. She flushes it and uses tissue paper to blow her nose and wipe under her eyes. She stands and opens the stall door.

She bumps past Gemma. Willow steps out of her way.

Simone tries really hard but she can't get all the soap off her hands. When she meets Gemma's reflection in the mirror, her eyes well with tears. Gemma's face is all concern. Simone drowns out the sound of her own heartbeat with the hand dryer.

It fills space in their conversation.

Gemma puts her arm around Simone's shoulders. Simone softens into the hug. "I'm sorry," she says.

"I forgive you."

It is so simple, but Gemma's quick forgiveness and unconditional love quiet Simone's heart. She calms down. Breathes easy. Until she sees Willow's shoes, and just by how she is standing, Simone can read her face. "Please don't big sister me, Willow. I know I've made this bed. I know I have to sneak out of it while Ficklow is sleeping."

Willow's crosses her ankles and leans against the wall. "As long as you bring a change of clothes."

"I plan to quit someday, not get fired. There will be no walk of shame. Enough with the metaphor of me being in bed with Ficklow. It's gross."

Willow shrugs. "He's gross."

"Totally, but I can't risk my professional future by burning a bridge. I want to go out in a blaze of glory, but I don't want to blow anything up."

"I'll take your word for it. I know in the past, you haven't had the best luck with partnerships panning out."

"That's why this job is just a transition. I'm under no illusion that Ficklow will ever make me partner or even give me any credit of note."

Willow nods. "Ficklow has shown his true colors and you have lost more than one good night of fun wallowing in a bottle of wine because of it. Aurora's right. Hire help for this crazy part of Ballistic Bride's order and call it good. It will make the rest of life easier to have someone who can help you."

"But I'm hesitant to hire someone. My label is so small. I barely make any money. I'm almost losing money on this order already. I'm focused on getting the pictures and using them for marketing. That's the deal with her. I don't want to piss off Ballistic Bride, but I also don't want to hire help before I'm established. The label is so new it doesn't even have a name. I just write *Bonhomme* on the invoices." Simone slumps against the sink. She winces when water seeps through her pants and makes a wet mark on her ass.

Willow steps closer to hold her by the shoulders. She touches their foreheads together. "Simone, I'm not talking about the rest of your life. This isn't about marrying someone."

Simone winces. Willow holds her still.

"I'm talking about a contract employee for one project, which will likely take less than a week."

Simone looks at Willow. Her advice feels like a dare. It reminds her of the way it felt when Aurora taunted her about her dislike for sharing responsibility.

Gemma wipes a rogue tear off Simone's cheek. "Let's go sit back down. You need food."

Nausea floods her again at the thought of food.

"Trust me. It will make you feel better. There's a salad bar now. I'll put something fresh together for you. Have you been living off of toast again?"

Simone grins a little sheepishly, and Gemma guides her back to their table.

3

*W*ithin a matter of hours a guy named Logan Clearwater answers Simone's ad. He doesn't attach a resumé. He just writes one line—"Hey, I'm your man."—and leaves his phone number. Not sure what to think, but somehow reassured by his lack of credentials and cryptic reply to her barebones request for a sewing minion, Simone takes a chance and dials the number.

"This is Logan," a man answers after the first ring. His voice is really deep.

"Um, hi." She clears her throat feeling tentative. "This is Simone. I'm calling to talk to Logan?" She cringes when that comes out like a question.

"This is Logan." There is a hint of wariness as he repeats his name, like someone used to hedging until they get the lay of the land.

"Um, right, this call is about the Craigslist ad you answered."

"Hey," the voice relaxes, "great!" It is early, but it sounds like he is in a crowded place. Gym shoes squeak and guys erupt in both cheer and objection. Voices dim as he continues, "So what is this project you need help with?"

Nice question. She had expected him to want to know what the job pays first.

"Well, it's just some really simple sewing, but there's a lot of it. Do you have any formal education?"

"None."

"But you can measure and cut accurately?"

"Yes."

"Do you know how to use an iron?"

"Of course." His tone is starting to sound mock official, like these questions amuse him. They amuse Simone, too.

"And you can use a sewing machine?"

"Yes."

"Do you have your own?"

"I do. I also own a serger." Logan pauses here. "Why? Will I be working at home? Is this piecework, or will I be working with you at your business?"

Suddenly, it occurs to Simone that hiring someone will mean just that: either they take the supplies and pattern and go about it unsupervised, which is a serious investment in materials, an insane trust in meeting deadlines, and a frightening lack of quality control, *or* she invites some stranger into her home.

"Um," Simone stammers, "I think I'd prefer it, if I hired you, that you bring your machine here and sew with me."

Ack. I never have strangers here, must prepare accordingly.

"Awesome."

"Great."

"Wait," she yells because it sounds like he is going to hang up. "We need to schedule an interview. Can you come by at six?"

"In the morning?" Logan asks.

"No." *God, no.* "This evening."

"Sure. Would you like me to bring my machine? I'm most

comfortable sewing on it, but I'm pretty good with something new. It's your preference. My grandmother couldn't stand another woman using her machines."

Simone smiles. *This is a good sign.* "Bring your own."

Simone gives Logan directions to her house and hangs up.

She closes her laptop and dials Aurora's number while she walks outside. It is still early in the day and a little chilly, but fresh.

"Yo, lady," Aurora answers. It sounds like she has been up all night. "What time is it?"

"Nine thirty."

"Shit."

"Been up all night?"

"I have photo packages for two weddings due tomorrow. Neither is done."

"Which two?"

"Denver and Flint, Michigan."

"Aurora, only you can make a wedding in Flint sound cool."

"Hey, it was cool!" Aurora clears her throat. "Why are you calling? It's early."

"I got an awesome C.L. response this morning."

"Do tell."

"He wrote one line."

"Really?" Aurora coughs. "Did he ask what the pay is?"

"No. He just wrote, 'Hey, I'm your man,' and left his name and number."

Aurora's laugh is husky and thick. "You called him, right?"

"Naturally."

"Soooo..."

"I'm interviewing him today at six." Her tone is smug, satisfied.

"Okay," Aurora yawns into the phone. "Call me when he leaves. My deadline is five for both assignments, so I'll need to decompress."

"Will do." Simone hags up the phone and exhales.

She arranges the pleats in her sheer curtain so it hangs evenly. Across from her are two tables set in the corner like an L. Her swivel chair is in the center. On one table is her sewing machine, on the other is her serger—a machine she uses only for stretchy knit materials like t-shirts. A lot of people have sewing machines by way of hand-me-down.

But not a serger.

That was credential enough for the interview.

This isn't rocket science.

It's a matter of time. Simone needs at least a day for each bridesmaid dress, three for a bridal gown.

But for an order of garters this size, I need a full week.

Hiring help is the only way. Especially with Fashion Bolder coming up.

Unease rolls through her. It makes her get up and move. She sees her converted two car garage through a man's eyes, a stranger's eyes. Her apartment is wide open, and at the same time tiny and intimate. Her workbench is at the center of the room—it's the place where everything she makes begins. Simone flips on the track lighting. Even light fills the space. Everywhere she looks there are baskets full of color, and folded and stacked materials. Plants and pictures peak out on bookshelves and knickknacks line the rest of the open spaces.

On the other side of the workbench and the bar where clothes in process hang, is her bed, a very small bathroom, and an open clawfoot tub. A kitchen runs along the wall to her right with a small cafe table and two chairs. Above the table are floating shelves stacked with books and baskets. The bed is somewhat partitioned off from the rest of the space by dowels hanging around its perimeter and the colored scarves which cascade along them.

Simone takes in a deep breath. There is nowhere to hide.

Overwhelmed at the thought of having to change everything for a little help, Simone avoids actually doing any of it and mills around instead, puttering and putting things away, but not out of sight. Somewhere there is some part of her that wants nothing to do with hiding. If this is going to work, it's because it is going to work for her, it's going to fit her.

~

Later that day Logan rides his bike down Simone's alley. He slows his single speed, looking for numbers on garages. Midway down the block, he sees the back of Simone's place. She has painted her house numbers a different color from the others. The numbers 323 ½ in cadet blue hang from hooks along the fence. Rolling through a break in the picket, he steps off his bike and leans it against the brick wall of the two car garage.

He sees her porch, which is just the two lines of a driveway overgrown and occupied by a couple of chairs and a little table. Behind them is a big picture window where the garage door once was. The sun is low and shining through new cottonwood leaves. He looks inside and sees a woman at the sink. She looks nothing like what he imagined. He thought she'd be overly artsy, dressed eccentrically in all black and made up. But she isn't. The woman standing in this small building makes his breath catch. She is lit up with late sunshine. It spills over her soft white blouse with short sleeves and tight cuffs, then down over her simple skirt of blue muslin. She wears a light blue scarf in her short, dark hair. A necklace sparkles at her breast-bone. She is barefoot.

Logan steps into the glow and knocks on the open door.

"Ms. Bonhomme?"

"Logan?"

"Yes." He clears his throat. "Simone? Are you expecting

others for interviews?" he asks, slightly disappointed at the thought of competition.

"No, I just didn't hear a car."

"Rode my bike."

"Did you bring your machine?"

"I did." Logan watches dismay cross Simone's face. "But don't worry," he reassures her, "she didn't even rattle. This is my baby. I'd never harm her."

Logan smiles reassuringly because Simone looks uncomfortable. He takes off his hat, gesturing as if to welcome himself in.

Simone nods. "Pardon me. Please, come in." She wipes her hands on a towel and opens a cupboard door. "Have a seat." She gestures to the tiny round table. "I'm making tea. Would you like some?"

"I would. What do you have?" Logan enters the room and looks around. It smells faintly like peppermint and grapefruit. In a few seconds, he realizes this is no shop. It is a home. The shop just seems to be a natural part of the space. Late light fills the room and gives it a hot glow. Bright spots of color pop against dominant white. This room is clean and cozy. A hodgepodge of big rugs cover the cement floor of the garage, overlapping in places. He can see bits of thread fallen from the table have woven themselves deep into the thicker pile under her sewing machines. Immediately, he likes this detail. She chose to put the lushest rugs under her there, where she obviously spends a lot of time.

"I was going to make a pot of jasmine. Sound good?"

"Great." Logan sets his backpack down on her tidy workbench. He looks up and sees her curtained futon made up like a sofa. Immediately, he tries to quiet the surprise thoughts that start to race. He clears his throat. "May I use your bathroom to wash my hands?"

"Sure." Simone gestures behind the screen. "Sorry. The

toilet is in the closet." She shrugs her shoulders. "It will be cozy?"

"Cozy." Logan barely fits in the tiny water closet with enough room to slide the pocket door shut. He turns to lift up the lid and stops. The seat is wearing a pair of long, hot-pink fuzzy socks. He laughs. When he is finished washing his hands, he sits down to tea.

Logan struggles to get his legs under the table, and instead hovers around it like a giant. "So, what's with the socks?"

"Huh?" Simone looks at the socks she just put on: basic Argyle.

"On the toilet seat."

"Oh, well, it gets cold at night. This place doesn't have the best insulation."

Logan looks up. "It probably would cost less than a hundred bucks to fix that."

"It's almost summer."

"It will help keep it cool, too. Does the garage door still open?"

"No."

"We can put a fan in up there, to draw out the heat." Logan is talking on like a teenage girl. Simone has thrown him off, and he thanks heaven when she offers him a giant cinnamon roll and he can sink his teeth into it to avoid saying anything else.

She watches him carefully, crossing her legs and arms. In one hand she cradles the teacup. Logan follows her throat as she swallows a small sip. She interrupts his thoughts when she asks him a question.

"Where did you learn how to sew?"

"My grandmother taught me. Or she let me learn. She used to do alterations and custom sewing. She raised me while my mom worked to pay the bills."

"Do you sew for a living now? Or design?"

"I went to school for graphic design."

Logan almost holds his breath as Simone sorts through the information. He can tell it isn't enough for her, but he doesn't want to get into the messy details. He had intended to be a graphic designer, period. After his college girlfriend dumped him for his best friend, Logan turned all his focus to internships and grades. After college he began a lucrative small business working for high-level personal clients. But it morphed into something else when an idea he had took flight.

Simone takes another sip of tea. "Doesn't that take up most of your time?"

"It used to." Logan sits back slowly, not wanting to fold the chair beneath him. He decides to cut to the chase and not mince words about his employment. "I used to own my own company. Then I developed an app with my brother, which we sold for a good amount of money. Now I technically don't have a business anymore because my clients all phased out, and we've closed our sale. I'm sitting idle."

"What sort of app?"

"The kind that will take a person's handwriting and turn it into a font."

"I bet designers love that! It was probably a breeze to sell."

Logan nods, and enjoys the way her chocolate eyes warm up.

"So why do you want a sewing job?"

All of a sudden, Logan can't imagine not getting this job. He likes the sharp sweet woman sitting across from him. He chooses his next words with care and as much patience as possible. "Honestly?"

Simone nods in mild encouragement.

"I'm bored. It's simple, really. I don't need the money. I don't need a stressful job. I simply want to work with my hands and find a way to make beautiful things with beautiful people on a daily basis."

Again, Logan watches as Simone tastes her tea and looks across her space. "You could make your own clothes."

"I don't know much about menswear. Besides, I prefer to sew for women. They appreciate it more."

Simone blushes. "This job is really basic." She says it like it's a warning.

"Great. What is it?"

Simone gets up and pulls a basket from the shelf above her. Logan watches as her shirt lifts to reveal a thin band of skin above her skirt. She has a freckle next to her bellybutton. It is an effort to shift his attention back to what she is doing. Simone sets the basket in her lap. On the table between them she places a finished garter, some pale-peach satin, elastic, and thread.

"I suppose now is as good a time as any for your test."

Logan watches Simone's eyes glow a warmer shade of sepia with humor.

"Test?"

"Yep. Mimic this in twenty minutes or less."

Logan clears their dishes and stacks them in the sink before he washes his hands again and sets his machine up next to Simone's.

Simone puts her pincushion on the workbench.

Logan looks at her and winks. "Start the timer."

Simone leaves Logan alone to complete the test, and twenty minutes later he joins her on her porch. He tosses three garters into her lap and sits down. Simone looks them over, and he's confident about what she sees. The sizes are exactly the same. The stitching is clean and finished well. There isn't any twisting of the ties, which means he didn't force the material through his machine or hold on to it and pull against the feed. He's certain she cannot tell her original from his two copies.

She looks up. "I hate to do this, but...your hired. You are

going to be so bored. We have to make three hundred seventy-eight of these, plus a dozen spares."

"Who placed an order? The Rockettes?"

Simone cringes and tells him about Ballistic Bride. "Seriously, though," she says, "I don't really want to hire you and then have to hire someone else when you have died from tedium. Do you think you can commit to one week of serious effort?"

"Not a problem." Logan considers it too short a time to get to know Simone. Fishing for ways to change that, he asks, "Do you already have the materials?"

"I do, but there is one more thing. I didn't have you sew this on the sample, but every garter gets embroidered. The bride with her name and wedding date. Bridesmaids with their names, and the guest garters might get embroidered with guest names."

Logan takes in the ramifications of this detail. "*That* sounds like a nightmare."

"Quite."

Logan is not deterred by Simone's warning tone. He reaches for her hand and shakes it. "Thank you." Her palm is narrow, and her fingers close softly around his. "When do I start?"

4

*S*imone questions her decision to hire Logan Clearwater from the moment he leaves her studio. Standing at the back of her building watching him ride away on his bike doesn't do much to settle her mind.

He is way too accomplished.

His energy is enormous.

He's too tall for the space I have made.

And, he smells really good. Like sandalwood.

Simone holds her head. She can't imagine spending the next week cooped up inside her garage with him. All long limbs, lean and super strong, he is her kind of subtle sexy. He wears honest, clear blue eyes beneath the brim of his hat, and they caught her by surprise from the start. Whenever he got near enough to smell, she wanted him close enough to touch. From the moment he sat down at her table she had to focus hard on why he was there in the first place.

She almost didn't offer him the job, but there was no good reason why she shouldn't have. Her list of rambled objections held very little to justify finding someone else. Logan is qualified, has very good craftsmanship, and has no other job or project competing for his attention. A week or so of his time and focus are all she needs.

Just imagining it makes her stomach flip. Now that he has left, Simone sees evidence of him in all the little places: the chair at her table is askew, creases she hasn't made run through the carpet beneath her sewing table, and there are two cups and two saucers in the sink.

When she'd reached above him to get the basket, she had felt his eyes on her.

They'd felt good.

Different.

When he shook her hand, she immediately wondered what it would feel like to have his hands around her waist.

Would he like the way she is shaped? Would he want to hold her tight?

I need a boyfriend.

Who am I kidding?

I need a good lay.

Simone calls Aurora.

"Okay, spill the deets."

"He's definitely not gay."

"Most definitely?"

"Undeniably. From the moment he walked in the door, it felt like he had been here a thousand times before." She thinks about the way he made her blush. "He is too big a person to be comfortable in my garage. You should have seen him at my dining table."

"Mr. Big I'm Your Man." Aurora pulls this cheesy pun, and it makes Simone laugh. "Seriously, though, is he a fit?"

"He is a graphic designer who made money selling an app, so he's not helping me for the pay. He says it's for fun, and to occupy his time. But, he just seems too hot and hip to have free time."

"No sense making a call before you've spent some time

working with him. This is going to be remarkably good for you, Simone. I don't think in all the time I've know you have you willingly worked on a group project."

"This isn't school, Aurora, this is business. I'm his boss." As the words leave Simone's mouth, they feel like a lie. He was too familiar with her immediately for him to think of her as above him. And from the outside, it certainly seems impossible since she stands a foot shorter than him.

"Okay." Aurora's tone mocks Simone's thoughts. She knows better.

"Anyway, tonight I've got to crush Ficklow's entry for Fashion Bolder. And when Logan comes to work, I'm all about being the boss," Simone assures her. "This *is* business."

When she hangs up the phone, Simone's conviction wavers. She feels like she is on the verge of something unknown and monumental, like a precipice, like change, and it makes her uncomfortable.

She lights some candles and puts on some music. It takes effort to conjure the mood she needs to be in to come up with the Fashion Bolder entry James is looking for. Her time with Logan has shifted her energy completely into the realm of something softer and more magical than the sober style of Ficklow. It takes organizing her collection of fabric scraps by color to get her mind in the right space. Finally, she sits down with her pad of paper and a pencil and lets her hand and mind flow. Within a couple of hours, Simone has the sketches for one bridal gown and three bridesmaid dresses. After the dozen custom dresses she just designed and made for Ballistic Bride, these three dresses hardly seem like enough room for her to showcase talent or her best ideas.

James wants her best work.

Simone knows what she has done for him over the past three years has been good. Her designs have been mindful and the production efficient. She has kept the Ficklow brand intact and has also done wonders for improving his bottom line. The label has made a better profit since she came onboard. She is the only team member remaining after last quarter, for whatever reason, and she considers it a sign she is valued.

For years, she has endured and competed with coworkers for distinction. This entry is Simone's chance for her to meet Ficklow on his level as a designer. An artist. For her to prove that a promotion or recognition of some kind is in order. She feels like taking a risk with this opportunity.

Simone leafs through her drawing pad, analyzing the designs. They are what James expects, but they feel too staid, too boring to enter into a competition in the running for Berlin Fashion Week. They are on brand for Ficklow but completely lackluster.

Huffing, she gets up and makes a cup of tea. From across the room, she stares at the notepad. Her mind follows each of her alternatives to their natural end. She could do the safe thing, the one that will pass, and fly below the radar. Or she could go for it and push the edges of what Ficklow could be.

Why not give her imagination free rein and choose her submission with honesty once both are drawn up?

With conviction, she sets her teacup down and gets her tiny box of pot off the top shelf above her cafe table.

She sits outside under a blanket on her patio chair for fifteen minutes. The day has grown dark and chilly. Tiny twinkle lights run throughout the potted plants lining the perimeter of her porch. She studies a seam in the concrete, and it reminds her of the seams on the garters Logan sewed. He pulled two of them together in the time she'd hoped he'd complete one. This project is going to be a breeze if he sticks with it. She takes a deep breath, uncomfortable relying on someone else to get her across the finish line. Uncomfortable with the attraction she already feels for Logan.

Towering above her is a canopy of catalpa trees and an opening to the sky.

Through the gap, Simone can see stars. The town of Boldene is dark enough at night to see the constellations. They shine clearly above her and give her direction and peace.

Keep your head screwed on straight. Focus on the goal. One right move after another without distraction.

Stoned, Simone walks back inside with renewed perspective.

James left this entry up to me.

The only child in her thrives with distinction and independence. To be left alone to do what she does best. If this entry can give her more freedom without Ficklow hovering over her every stitch, it is worth the risk. Simone begins to draw a series of dresses she feels pushes the edges of Ficklow's tight boundaries. She sticks with his signature monochrome pallet of black, white, and gray, but loosens the lines and creates more flow than what is typical of the more severe and sharper edges of Ficklow's classics.

The results make her smile. They might not be what she would wear, but she does know women who would. She sets them out individually on her worktable. Next to each other they mesh well, and Simone can see a line of women wearing these dresses and walking down the runway in Berlin. Butterflies move through her guts at the thought of being backstage, readying everyone and making sure all the final details are in place. She can almost even see what it would be like to take the stage behind them and wave at the crowd in appreciation.

Almost.

~

All the romantic charm of yesterday and last night are lost by the time Simone meets with Ficklow in his office the next morning.

With ruthless efficiency James walks across the back wall of his office, pinning Simone's sketches to the Angie. Each time one of his thumbtacks pierces indelicately through the paper, Simone feels it in her fingertip like a blood test. It hurts in the itchiest way.

She can see what he dislikes before he's even turned around. She resists the impulse to gag when he sweeps his hand across his belt to push the lapel of his jacket back and stand with a hand on his hip, feigning deep thought.

Ficklow interrupts the silent list of flaws she stacks together in her mind with one she hadn't considered. "What are you thinking here by making the bride look fatter than she is with an empire waist?"

Simone holds still, resisting the impulse to point out the fact that there is no bride. They have no idea who the model will be or what she will look like. She edges around this by saying, "There is more material and more room to move in the empire waist than in some of our more signature designs. But I thought to give those with a different body type the opportunity to wear a Ficklow by highlighting other features."

Ficklow's lip curls with discomfort. His sleek designs have always looked best on sizes zero to four. "This bride would stick out like a sore thumb in our showroom. We have nothing like it."

Simone tries again. "Not necessarily. The fit is still slim and flattering. I avoided lace and chose silk and silk crepe for the fabrics. They are two of my favorites, and I know that you used them much more often in your earlier work. Perhaps it's time to give yourself a nod by bringing them back?"

Ficklow chews on this idea. Pacing back and forth looking at the designs.

"It looks like these folds just go wherever. There is no structure. I can't find the line."

"Inside the dresses there is less built-in support, no bodices, but that really isn't a concern since many brides these days prefer to wear some sort of full-body supportive undergarment."

Ficklow turns around slowly.

Simone finds the will power to continue despite the scowl on his face. "I've found this to be a big bonus when it comes to manufacturing and getting the shapes and sizes to be consistent and accurate. If we can avoid interior sewn-in supports our costs will go down considerably."

Ficklow walks back over to lean against his desk. He crosses his arms over his chest. Today, his suit is a deep plum purple, so dark it is hard to tell it's purple unless the light is just right. The lavender tie, however, erases all doubt. Simone finds his look so choreographed it's ripe.

She swallows and has a hard time getting past the lump in her throat. Sensitive fingertips pick at invisible lint on the hem of her dress.

Ficklow just lets her stew.

Finally, he says, "I asked for your best work. I'm not convinced this is it. I'm not convinced what you've put together was for me at all. Examine your priorities, Simone, and align accordingly. Or I will align them for you. You have one more chance to show me something good. Something I wouldn't be ashamed to submit under my label."

The phone on his desk rings. It deafens Simone and silences James.

He walks around the desk to answer it. When he recognizes the caller, he sits down and shoos Simone out of his office with his hand.

On numb legs, Simone walks to the cork board and retrieves her drawings. The taste of pennies fills her mouth. In the time it takes her to pull the door behind her, Simone overhears James talking about the competition. She closes it almost completely and leans her ear into the crack.

"I'm calling in my favor, Candy. I want a sure spot in the competition." James' voice is low and definitive. A pause follows. "I don't want to argue."

His chair creaks as he leans back. Simone imagines him preening like a crippled gorilla in the tight cut of his suit. She hopes his seams strain.

Immediately, Logan comes to mind, his movements solid and easy. He is a man who doesn't have to try to fill a room.

"Let me know what you need from me to make it happen." James waits for Candy to close the call.

Simone tries hard, but she can't hear anything of what might be going on at the other end of the line. The heavy thunk of the receiver settling into the cradle spurs her into action. Heart racing, she rushes on tiptoe to the bathroom and locks the door behind her.

Moments later, James knocks on the door as he walks by and shouts, "Piss, don't preen."

Simone washes her hands and presses the damp paper towel to her forehead and upper lip, fighting the sweat collecting there. It sounded like James just bullied his way into Fashion Bolder.

Feeling the pressure, she takes her designs back to her desk and stashes them in a drawer. She hunkers down to begin again, totally uninspired. She wishes she'd brought both sets of designs with her, but this morning she made the bold decision to take a chance and go with her more fluid designs. She made herself leave the other set at home so she wouldn't lose her nerve at the last minute and use the boring ones.

The minutes crawl by, and she hides from James, doing whatever she can to bide time until she can go home.

An hour before closing, Ficklow ushers someone through

from the front of the store to the back. She is tall, model thin, with straight blond hair past her waist, straighter teeth, and eyes a more interesting shade of hazel than Simone's brown.

Simone tries to smile, but this woman is intimidating.

James introduces her as Heidi Jones, their new teammate. Simone hadn't realized he'd started interviewing, but the thought of help with running the store is almost a welcome relief.

But watching James "orient" Heidi clarifies to Simone that she is there as more than a mere store clerk. Dressed in a black pencil skirt with a crisp white shirt, Heidi clearly will have no problem following the dress code. From the way she is smiling at Ficklow, she also won't have a problem greasing her path to team leader.

Suddenly spun around and questioning everything, Simone packs up her stuff and leaves early. Ficklow doesn't even flinch when she says she isn't feeling well, that she might not be in tomorrow. She isn't sure he's heard her say a word; he's too busy finding an angle to look down Heidi's blouse.

5

*A*s soon as Simone is around the corner and headed back toward the hill to her house, tears begin to blur her vision. She's annoyed by the sunset, by the incessant bird-song, by the optimism of spring. She is frustrated over why she gives two cents what Ficklow thinks. Her hands and arms feel weak, and she doesn't have the energy to climb on her bike. She stops and gets off it. Instead of pressing on, she takes a shortcut and heads for Aurora's apartment.

Aurora answers the door with a cigarette hanging from her faded red lips.

"Hey, Sim, come on in. I'm Skyping with a client, but I'll be done in a minute."

Simone follows Aurora to her dining room table and sits down. The table is littered with papers and an overflowing ashtray. Aurora's Mac is open, and the little apple glows at Simone. The computer is the only light in the darkening room; clearly, Aurora has been working here all day.

Aurora takes a long drag and moves her mouse. "Okay, Jen," she exhales a huge lungful of smoke, "where were we?"

Aurora continues her conversation, and Simone stands up.

She turns on the cozy overhead lamp and picks up the ashtray. She takes it out onto the balcony and empties it in a big coffee can. She leans against the railing, looking out, and notices a cottonwood tree loaded with buds. She looks down; on the grass below are tons of tiny twigs. The squirrels are at it early this year. It always seems like such a shame...all those potential leaves will never unfurl because some little furry rodent nibbled at a sweet knot and broke the twig's connection.

Aurora leans against the railing beside her. "What's up?"

Simone turns to face her. "I need therapy."

"Therapy?" Aurora puts her cigarette out in the ashtray Simone still holds.

"Yep, the real deal."

"You're lucky, sister. If you'd asked for real food, I would have offered you pickles. But ask for ice cream, and I've got you covered. Whiskey, too."

Back inside, Aurora grabs the ice cream, two spoons, a bottle of Jameson, and two shot glasses. She uncaps the bottle and pours them each a shot. She passes one to Simone, they toast, and toss the whiskey back. Simone holds her glass out, and Aurora raises her dark eyebrows. She pours each of them another shot; they toast and drink. Simone sets her glass down and picks up the ice cream.

Aurora drags two chairs together on her balcony and they sit down. After a few minutes of silence, Simone swaps pints with Aurora and begins to tell her about her day. She gets to the part where James brought Heidi through to the back.

"Uh-oh."

Simone nods. She feels a little better; the whiskey makes her warm and nearly comfortable.

"The funny thing is," she continues, "the whole time he was walking around his office, decimating me, I was mentally very there. But another part of me kept comparing him to Logan."

38

"Now?" Aurora holds up a hand, palm out to pause the conversation. "Are we going to talk about Logan?"

Simone nods and Aurora stands. "I'm goin' for three. You in?"

Simone shrugs. "Might as well. One for the body, two for the head, three for the heart."

Aurora returns to the balcony, third shots in hand.

"To our hearts, may they be forever buoyed by Jame-o."

Simone sets her empty glass down and is grateful she lives just around the corner. The third shot hits her hard, and before she knows it, the ice cream is gone.

"Oh, Sim," Aurora hugs her, "you need some afternoon delight."

"I know. I said as much to myself yesterday." Simone sits back and really sees what is going on with Aurora. "You, on the other hand, are glowing."

"Right. I've been awake for forever."

Simone isn't dissuaded. She gives Aurora time to sit under her careful watch. Aurora does not disappoint her. There is a tiny bit of blush that isn't whiskey induced on her friend's cheeks. "Did you get together with your getaway lover?"

Aurora lifts her chin. "I did."

Simone trusts Aurora implicitly. "What is it like to have someone you get to see only on scheduled time, for hot sex and adventure, and then you are free to live your life as you see fit otherwise?"

Aurora carefully replies. "Worth it."

"Do you ever want something more?" Simone has a hard time imagining Aurora ever settling down.

Aurora stands up. "It is more than I want already."

Simone turns toward Aurora. "Is it?"

Aurora stares into the stars. "I have a hard time juggling everything sometimes. Before this distraction, it was just work and my mom."

"How is your mom?"

"The same. She's still a bit nuts and unpredictable. But I'm grateful her friend Tilly is living with her now."

"Doesn't it make life more intense to do the PI work on top of it all?"

"It does, sometimes, but mostly it relieves the intensity. It gives my life perspective to see others living theirs."

"What are the jobs you love the best?"

"Impersonator assignments."

"What do you mean?"

"Where someone is pretending to be someone else for whatever reason. Most of the time it begins pretty innocently. Like a fake name at a bar to pick up a one-night stand. But sometimes those things get spun and sticky. And people do crazy things around illicit affairs and to cover them up."

Simone follows Aurora back inside, and three steps across the threshold she gets an idea. "That sounds like a lot to manage."

Aurora looks over her shoulder. "It is. Not everyone is cut out for it. That's how I get hired. Someone slips up and the people they love need to know more. It isn't dangerous until someone gets hurt."

"I'd be the only one getting hurt, or rather my reputation would be."

Aurora puts a hand on Simone's shoulder. "Earth to Sim. What are we talking about?"

Simone starts to think out loud. "What if my way out of Ficklow were a little convoluted? Winning the Fashion Bolder competition for myself would give me just the leg up I would need in this first year of business. The funding, the exposure, and, most importantly, the opportunity to be on the runway in Berlin.

"In my contract with Ficklow, I have just enough room to hang myself. This day job was supposed to bridge a gap, but, lately, I find myself slipping into the familiar pattern of wanting to please and be recognized. I'm growing Ficklow's business when I should be growing my own. I'm a solopreneur. I have to get out of there, or I'm going to let yet another pivotal opportunity pass me by."

"What are you thinking?"

"There isn't any harm in just entering, is there? I mean, there is no guarantee that my submission would be admitted to the competition, right? I might not ever have to worry about all these what ifs, but if I don't try, I'll always wonder if I would have gotten in on my own."

Aurora nods her head. "Obviously, Ficklow knows *Bonhomme*. Are you thinking you want to submit under an alias?"

"It would have to be an alias label, for sure, and I'd need different contact information, a completely separate email and phone number because I'm already listed as contact on the submission for Ficklow Fashion."

Simone's mind is whirling, and she feels just drunk enough to believe this is a good idea. There are a lot of things to determine and moving parts to align, but if she can make the details work, this might be the risk worth taking. She needs freedom, and Ficklow's hold feels like a vise until her student loans are paid and her business makes enough. Without a win like this that could take years.

6

$\mathcal{S}$imone wakes up the next morning feeling particularly horrible. She slept in her clothes, on top of her covers, huddled under a couch throw. She sends Ficklow an email confirming she's taking a sick day and guilt immediately floods her system in a cold sweat. She knows it isn't right to run from the discomfort at work, and part of her can see she's taking a big risk not coming in today with another set of designs. To make good on her time away from the office she sends Logan an email asking if he is free to work today.

Twenty minutes of hot water in the shower isn't enough to rid her neck of the ache from sleeping cold. She puts on a pair of soft sea-green velour pants, her dad's old gray Henley, and a giant cardigan. She uses a bright blue scarf to tie the sweater closed, overlapping it around her waist. In a blue hat, a pair of wool socks and heavy slippers she pads her way over to the kitchen sink.

The morning is cold and gray. Simone is hung over. Sighing because she remembers what she told Aurora, Simone rubs her lips and gets busy making coffee. She needs at least three mugs of hot brew before she will consider the day. A big glass of warm water lands like a heavy stone in her empty stomach. It makes her nauseous. She flips on the coffeemaker and finds the tin on her shelf. She lights her one-hitter and walks over to the big glass garage door. She draws the curtains aside and watches as rain begins to fall. It makes dark dots on the two tracks of cement leading to her doors. Her porch is at first polka dotted, then a dark, shiny satin gray.

Mr. Coffee sputters, and Simone returns to the kitchen. She fills a mug and drinks the first cup just leaning against the counter. She pushes her kitchen curtains aside and watches it rain on the grass through the little window over her sink. Surrounded by trees, she has a remarkable amount of privacy. When she refills her cup, she takes it with her to the table. She opens her computer and checks her Etsy conversations. Ballistic Bride has sent her word on the guest garters. It is not what she hopes to hear. It isn't at all what she expects to hear.

A knock on the window shocks Simone into looking up. Logan is at the door.

"Shit." Simone hits a button and sends the conversation to the printer on a shelf above. She stands up, and another wave of nausea hits her. She cringes and opens her door.

Logan stands there in the rain holding a pastry bag. Blue eyes smiling beneath the brim of his dripping hat. "Morning," he says and his dimples form a perfect set of parentheses around his lips.

"It is, isn't it?" Suddenly, Simone realizes what she is wearing and it makes her shift her feet.

"Everything good?" Logan draws out the word. "Do you still want to work today? I got your email while I was at the coffee shop."

Simone looks down at her hangover costume and nods. "I think we have to." She steps aside to let Logan in.

He hands her the pastries, then takes off his wet shoes and puts them in one of the cubbies behind the door.

"Do you feel okay?" he asks again.

Simone answers frankly, "Like a good boss, I called in sick to my day job because I got drunk last night. I'm hungover and," she goes for it, "a little stoned."

She pours him coffee and hands him the mug.

Logan takes a sip and nods. He pulls four brownies out of the bag and stacks them on a plate. "Pot is the only way to cure a hangover. That and a greasy plate of eggs and potatoes. Or second best," he turns to her and offers her the plate, "a hot dark delight."

He has a cute lopsided grin that stretches out when Simone registers his words.

"A hot dark delight?" She blushes and an ache starts low in her belly.

He motions with the plate. "Midnight breakfast brownies with a kick of cayenne pepper. I hope you like spicy."

Immediately, Simone's mind goes to racy thoughts. She can't help it.

Hot, dark, delight, midnight, spicy...

Damn.

Simone coughs. She tugs down the edges of her hat and plucks a brownie off the stack.

Logan pulls out the chair opposite Simone's computer and sits down. She takes a big bite and hands him the printed conversation. He reads. She chews.

"This cannot be real." Logan finishes reading. "Are you serious?"

"I am. Or, apparently, she is." Simone leans back from the table and crosses her legs. Her floppy slipper brushes Logan's shin. She can't see any bit of the chair he sits on. She needs to keep an eye out for something man-sized and foldable.

Even though he is head and shoulders taller than her, she isn't intimidated by his size. Taking him in, she realizes she is

44

reassured by it. And his good humor. And right now, she'd like to be folded up in him.

Logan shuffles the pages again, looking at them with amusement. "Ballistic Bride has chosen gray fabric for her guest garters because she wants them embroidered with fifty different words for gray."

Simone accepts the papers and finds the list of synonyms. She clears her throat. "Gray, charcoal, smoke, ash, silver, cloud, gunmetal, steel, nickel, sterling, lead, gray hound, wolf, polar, stone, star, smut, soot, shadow, gravity, grit, grime, dust, porpoise, koala, elephant, mouse, pewter, revere, graphite, skyscraper, fog, oatmeal, owl, nimbus, halo, kingfisher, goose down, pigeon, aluminum, tin."

"That's only forty-two." Logan shocks Simone with the proof of his attention. "Do we have to come up with the last eight?"

"I suppose we do." Simone sets the list down.

"What girl would want a garter with the label 'oatmeal' or 'porpoise' embroidered on it? Talk about setting the wrong mood. Maybe Ballistic Bride needs to rethink this one. Have you responded yet?"

Simone shakes her head. "I haven't. I just read it. The idea seems initially way too stupid to comment on immediately. Maybe it's an inside joke? I could have slipped and given her my true opinion, and I need this order to turn out well, so I have to let her down diplomatically."

"I can help you." Logan pulls out his laptop and opens a word document. "We can type it up here so there is no risk of us sending something we don't want her to read. You dictate, I'll type. Just have at it on this first draft."

Simone looks at Logan and considers him. He is serious. His fingers are poised over the keyboard awaiting her words. She laughs. "No way."

"Yes way. Do it. Speak." He closes his eyes, waiting for her to begin. When she doesn't say anything right away, he prompts her. "Dear Ballistic Bride...whatever your real name is."

"Dear Ballistic Bride," Simone echoes, loving the way his eyebrows frame his eyes.

Logan types.

Simone recrosses her legs. "I just read through your last conversation about the guest garters." She pauses, and Logan motions for her to continue. "Your request is batshit crazy. Do you think the words 'aluminum' and 'elephant' put your guests in the mood to hookup?" Logan smirks at her and she blushes, hard. "Who would want a garter embroidered with the word 'grit' or 'grime' as memorabilia from your wedding?"

Wait. Those words just sounded sexy. Grit and grime. Not a turn off...?

"Wait," Logan echoes her thoughts and his fingers stop. He looks at Simone. "This might work."

Simone nods, every part of her responding to the words he isn't saying out loud.

"Grime." Logan pauses to think.

Simone likes how he doesn't hide what goes through his mind. It doesn't feel like there is any calculation behind the things he says.

"Fifty shades of gray might not be so bad, especially since she originally said she wanted guest names."

Simone agrees. It might be a kitschy idea, but it *is* memorable, a hell of a lot easier than names, and it seems Ballistic Bride might have a sense of humor. "Okay, I'll confirm it. Start thinking of some more words for gray."

"Majestic, mercury, mushroom." Logan starts jotting down his words. "No, mushroom sucks. Psilocybin is better. Wet concrete. Hey, are we going to get these approved by her?" Logan starts jotting down his words.

"Good point. I'll ask about it in the convo. It would be nice if you could just come up with the rest before I'm done typing. I'll list them at the bottom." Simone is sort of joking, but Logan takes her seriously.

"Pebble, bone, blade." Logan looks up in thought, fingers poised above his keys.

Simone stares at his Adam's apple. It is actually attractive.

Logan snaps his head down and comes up with the final three. "Mud, slip, clay. There. Not brilliant, but worth the first round of negotiations."

Simone chuckles and rewraps her sweater. "Okay, repeat."

Logan repeats the list carefully. Then he leaves Simone to finish the email while he clears their plates and puts on his shoes.

"I'll go get my stuff. Be back in a minute."

Simone nods, and Logan steps out into the rain.

Through the big glass window she watches Logan open the hatch to an SUV. It's sort of funny to see such a big man tuck an iron under his jacket and hoist a board out with his other hand. Logan leans against the car and bumps it closed. Drops fall from the trees above into his hair and down his face. He walks back inside and for the next few hours they sew and share easy conversation.

A second knock at the door startles Simone. She was distracted, wondering what Logan's skin would have tasted like if she had licked the drops of rain through the stubble on his cheeks.

Aurora knocks again—she's at the glass garage door peering in. Simone sees the moment Aurora's eyes land on Logan, her dark eyebrows jump high above her unnecessary sunglasses. Through the window she finds Simone and nods once. Before Simone can get to the door, Aurora opens it. She stands inside, dripping wet, still looking over her lenses at Logan.

"Hey, Sim," she casually says and shrugs out of her black leather jacket. She kicks off her Doc Martins, and they land in the corner.

"Hey." Simone hands her a yellow dishtowel, and hangs her jacket up.

Logan stops cutting and turns to face the girls. He leans against the cutting table, forgetting it is just a door propped up on sawhorses. The door shifts, and he reaches back to catch it before it tips, making himself laugh.

Aurora whispers to Simone, "There is a real man in this garage. Introduce me."

"Logan Clearwater," Simone begins, "this is, Aurora Copper. Aurora, this is my employee, Logan." Simone emphasizes the latter while eying Aurora.

Logan steps forward and extends a hand. "Nice to meet you."

Aurora shakes his hand with a smile. "Nice to meet you, too."

Logan turns back to the table and resumes working. Aurora grabs Simone's elbow and mouths, "What the fuck?"

Simone mouths back, "I told you so."

Regaining her composure, Aurora clears her throat and says, "I just stopped by to see if you were among the living, and to run some ideas past you, Sim, if you have the time?"

"I can take a few minutes. Logan, you don't mind, do you?"

Logan shakes his head. The girls sit down at Simone's little table, and Aurora opens her laptop.

"Hey, by the way," Simone whispers, "sorry about last night. But thank you so much for the therapy."

"Clearly, you needed it." Aurora winks and turns her computer so Simone can see some photos. They spend a few minutes going over the details of Aurora's latest job, and Simone gives her some feedback. The meeting takes about a half an hour, and when they are done Logan stops cutting.

"That's it," Logan says. "The gray is all cut. One color, fifty shades."

Simone scoffs and begins to count them out. The scarf

around her waist slips loose. Logan catches it with his fingers. He steps closer to draw the scarf around her and retie it. He smells clean and fresh, but not like a cologne. More like an essential oil or soap, something sandalwood or frankincense. When he ties the loop beneath her belt, his hands stay close, caught against her tummy.

Simone lifts her head.

Logan looks down at her and slowly smiles.

Aurora clears her throat and shoves her laptop back into her bag. "Well, that's it for me. Looks like you two have your hands full."

Simone snaps to the present moment, and she can feel her cheeks turn a bright shade of pink.

Logan is so good natured that he chuckles and asks, "Do you need a ride somewhere? I have my car."

"No, thanks." Aurora grins. "I'm just around the corner. Besides, I can see you are needed here."

Simone hands Logan the squares and then clenches her jaw as she walks her friend out the door. Aurora pauses to give her a pointed *I-saw-that* look. Simone's eyes widen at the reproach and then roll with the encouragement when Aurora fans herself.

Simone waits in the rain watching her friend cross the backyard. Her sweater is snug and warm, tied tight around her waist.

7

*L*ogan leaves Simone's apartment with a brighter attitude than the weather would suggest. By the time they finished for the day, it had grown nearly dark. Now the streets of Boldene are slick, and stoplights shine in the reflections. He takes the backroads through town to pick up Reggie for poker.

It has been so long since Logan felt this way, it hurts to remember it. His chest aches a little; his thoughts are distracted.

The light turns green.

Before he knows it, Logan has pulled up in front of his brother's apartment building. He puts his hands to his face and takes a deep breath. He can still smell the grapefruit and peppermint permeating Simone's studio. Her home. That incredibly intimate space. Her smell is more intense on his hands so he puts them back on the wheel. It's been nearly a decade since Logan allowed another woman to pique his interest like Simone just did.

Since college, Logan has only been focused on work and

Reggie. Even though Reggie is already twenty-one, Logan still thinks of him as thirteen. He can still picture his younger brother standing in the driveway of their beat-up duplex, a basketball in one hand, staring at the taillights of their mom's car as she drove away. That was the last time they saw her. They hear from her every now and then but haven't seen her since the day she left. Logan has been looking out for his kid brother ever since, and it hasn't been easy. Reggie was full of resentment initially when their mom didn't come home, and, even now, he doesn't speak to her when she calls. He asks Logan how she is to make sure she's okay, because he's a good kid and all heart, but he doesn't engage.

Logan has no resentment toward his mom. Something in her broke when his dad died, and then his grandmother passed away within a few years of that. Logan was old enough to see how alone his mother felt. When Reggie's dad came along, it brought new energy and gave his mother renewed purpose. But Reggie's dad wasn't there to stay. Wild from the start he was more of an adventure for his mom than anything, and soon it was the three of them on their own. There were boyfriends and empty promises, but more and more their mother spent time "out." When his mom took the car that night and didn't come back before daylight, Logan had just turned eighteen and was doing most of the providing anyway.

If it weren't for *Antiques Roadshow* and computer science, Reggie might not have made it through his teens alive. Logan did his best, but in college himself and working at the same time, he by no means parented Reggie. At the most, he kept him fed and tried to keep him out of jail and if not in school, at least learning something. Giving him the project of writing code for the app they sold had worked wonders. It gave Reggie the challenge of producing something practical and generating revenue. There was a lot he taught himself to make it work. For all of Reggie's book knowledge, Logan knows if it were up to him, he'd be treasure hunting and living out of a bag, pursuing his Indiana Jones fantasies.

"Yo, bro." Reggie slides into the passenger side of Logan's car wearing a hoodie pulled over his head. His damp sneakers squeak on the floorboards.

"What's up, Tripp?" Logan hits his mark, and Reggie cringes at the nickname. Logan laughs.

"What's up with you? Why so fresh?"

Logan shrugs. "I feel good."

"Where were you today? I drove by earlier."

"Started my new job."

Reggie chuckles. "Okay, what's the new job?"

For the first time since leaving Simone's, Logan feels uneasy. "Don't judge, okay?"

Reggie looks incredulous.

"I picked up some side work sewing."

Reggie starts to laugh, but the cautionary look Logan throws shuts him up. "But you haven't done that in..."

"Forever. It just comes back, though."

"Like riding a bike." After a few minutes of silence, Reggie says, "I wish I could have had more time with grandma."

Logan wishes he had, too. "She was a classy lady."

Logan keeps this part of the conversation short. They are getting really near the topic of their mother, Reggie's least favorite thing to talk about.

Finally, Reggie seems to register what Logan is saying. "Wait, why did you pick up side work sewing?"

"I'm bored out of my mind."

"But we have these deals going down with Svere and Devon!"

"That stuff is all talk and paperwork. It isn't tangible. If I can't see what I'm making with my eyes and feel it eventually with my hands, then it isn't work."

"For heaven's sake, start a garden! Get a hobby!"

"Sewing is a hobby. At least it is a skill I'm not willing to let go to waste."

Reggie shifts to face Logan. "There has to be a catch. What are you sewing?"

Logan's unease returns. "Garters."

"Gators, like, for mountaineering?" Reggie's interest is piqued.

"No." Logan hesitates. "Garters."

"As in lingerie." Reggie draws out the French for emphasis.

Logan nods and pulls over in front of Svere's house.

Reggie smiles. "Women's underwear. This is starting to make sense. Who are you working with?"

There is no stopping the enormous grin that explodes across Logan's face.

"X marks the spot."

Before Reggie can terrorize him with further questions, Logan gets out and shuts the car door.

"Hey." Reggie chases him up the walkway.

Logan reaches the porch and spins on his heel. With arms outstretched he asks, "What?"

Then Svere Benhaus opens his front door and envelops Logan in a hug. Svere and Logan first met each other through their mutual friend, Adam Bear, who owns The Salt Lick. They have been playing basketball and poker once a week together for years ever since.

"Hey, Pretty Boy," Reggie says and hugs Svere.

"Keep calling me names, Squirt. I'm taking all your money tonight." Svere hugs Reggie back.

"Whatever." Reggie ducks out of the headlock Svere tries. "You are too manicured for getting dirty."

Logan adds to the ribbing of Svere. "He's right. Did you just return from the salon?" Tall, golden-blond, model-maintained, and hipster cool, Svere outclasses their group of friends. But they tolerate him—he brings in the girls.

And he's smart as fuck.

Logan appraises his friend. "Bro, there is something different about you."

Svere clenches his jaw, suppressing a smile.

"What the hell? You both are all girl crazy." Reggie says and pushes past Logan and Svere heading for the kitchen.

Svere replies in an even tone, "What? I just got back from California. Had some business there."

He joins Reggie in his newly remodeled kitchen. Reggie talks into the fridge. "Unless the 'business' has anything to do with biofuels, then I'm not interested."

Logan follows. "Reggie, let it go. We aren't talking work right now."

Reggie cracks open a beer. "Fine. Svere, your place looks great. The remodel makes this kitchen feel twice as big." He rolls his eyes and motions on and on with his hand.

Svere bats his pretty eyes and says, "How kind of you to notice." He takes them on a short tour around the bungalow, until they are interrupted by the doorbell.

Adam Bear greets everyone after he empties his hands into the refrigerator. Adam and Logan are about the same height, and when they shoot hoops, he usually pairs with Reggie. That makes the teams nearly even and gives them lots of room for roasting and ribbing.

After the usual round of greetings and collectively hazing Reggie, the guys settle in around the kitchen table. Once the cards are dealt and Logan, Reggie, Svere, and Adam have fallen into the rhythm of Texas Hold'em, Reggie starts to talk.

He dances around the topic. Logan can feel him resisting the urge to dive right in. He prepares himself for what is to come. He hasn't had the hots for a girl since a singular dive-bomb rebound post-College Angie.

"What's her name?" Reggie finally gets down to it. When he speaks, the whole table goes quiet.

Logan plays his cards and avoids eye contact.

Svere casually asks, "Whose name?"

Logan can feel Reggie's eyes on him.

Reggie was a kid when Angie crushed Logan's heart. He's been protective ever since.

"Simone."

Adam perks up. "Bonhomme?"

Logan winks. "You know her?"

Adam's eyes open wide. "There aren't that many Simones in Boldene. One of my cocktail waitresses is best friends with Simone."

Svere studies Adam. "Do you mean Gemma?"

Adam wipes his mustache and barely nods. Logan wonders what that nod means. "Bear, how well do you know her?"

Adam picks up his beer and takes a good drink. "She's solid. A very good friend to Gemma, but she works too much. She comes in on Blues Night to let off steam. Apparently, her boss is an asshole."

Logan takes in this new information. The soft and sparkly woman he spent the day with was tired, but she claimed to be just hungover. Being overworked by a jerk feels like a never-ending hangover. "No wonder she's hired help."

Adam wins the hand and pulls the chips toward him. "From what I've gathered, she's wanted to quit her job since she started."

Logan accepts the beer Svere hands him. "Why doesn't she go all in on her label—she has orders big enough to hire help?" These things are so cut and dry for Logan. Whenever he hasn't been happy at a job, he's moved on, or better yet, started his own thing.

Adam shrugs. "Chicks."

But that doesn't sit well with Logan. He saw the projects in development hanging behind Simone's workbench. There is no reason why she shouldn't be selling well in some way on her own.

Reggie interrupts his ideas before they get rolling. "I can see those wheels churning, brother. This might not be your problem to solve. Beware of perceiving a damsel in distress where there is none."

"I agree." Adam chuckles. "From what Gemma tells me, Simone is strung tight and fiercely independent. She doesn't ever think she needs help or advice."

Logan asks, "Where are the women capable of letting go just enough to trust a man to be a man?"

Svere diffuses Logan's frustration by punching Adam in the shoulder. "Pretty tight with Gemma these days."

"We work together a lot. I spend more time with her than anyone else. You start to tell each other stuff when that happens."

Svere nods. "Yeah, and remind me again who sets the schedule at your bar?"

Adam goes stone-cold silent. Logan takes pity and asks him if Simone has a boyfriend.

"Like I said, she's great. Just not great with men. She's been single since I've known her. Gemma said something about being left at the altar when they were young."

Logan's eyebrows go up. "How ironic that she spends her career designing bridal wear."

Adam shrugs. "I don't know the details. I just know what I've heard secondhand." He gets up and finishes his beer. "I feel like a girl for gossiping. Stop asking me questions. I'm going outside to smoke. Who's in?"

Everyone joins him. When he hands the joint to Logan a question occurs to him. "The pay is probably shit. What made you take the job?"

"She has this freckle..." Logan points near his belly button.

Svere whistles on an exhale and dogs start to bark in the neighborhood.

8

The next day, Simone wrestles the door to Ficklow Fashion open with one hand, the other set of drawings for Fashion Bolder tucked under her arm. She's crabby but well put together. After Logan left yesterday, she had to make peace with a new schedule. The order for Ballistic Bride is creeping into every corner of her life. Last night she was supposed to be free to simply come up with her own entry for Fashion Bolder. The fantasy entry, the one that is just for her. But when it was time to draw, when she had finished tidying up her space and setting everything in motion, nothing came. Nothing but the need to plot and plan a way to squeak in another dress for Ballistic Bride.

And when she's frank with herself, she acknowledges that Logan has surprised her. He is competent, and easy on the eyes as well as charming as can be. She looks forward to the time they spend together. It's something she thinks about often. It sneaks up on her, a sensation of something good in life that takes her a minute to put her finger on. It stands in stark contrast to the dread of coming back into work today.

Inside, she dumps her bag unceremoniously into her desk

chair. Lip gloss and other junk falls out and onto the floor beneath her desk. Grateful the office is empty, she drops to her knees and gathers her things. A giggle sounds from the confines of Ficklow's office. Not surprised, Simone stands and tugs her skirt smooth. Dreading what is coming next, she procrastinates by aligning the cover of her designs and brewing coffee.

At precisely nine o'clock she rounds the corner and finds his office door open. He's there, of course.

With Heidi.

She checks her watch to make a show of knowing she isn't late.

"I'm sorry to interrupt. James, will you let me know when you and Heidi are finished?"

"No need. Heidi is joining us this morning."

Wondering what the hell is going on, Simone walks through the door and sits in the only open chair.

"You weren't feeling well yesterday, and I wasn't sure when you'd be back. Time is of the essence as you know. So, I asked Heidi to come up with an entry of her own. Sort of a welcome-to-the-team challenge."

While Simone doesn't envy the position James put Heidi in, she does envy the cool Heidi has under pressure. She is dressed in another flattering heather-gray pencil skirt with fitted blazer and silk blouse. Simone adjusts the standing neckline and tie of her chiffon blouse and wonders if she should have shied away from the black-on-white polka dot pattern. Next to the sleek composure Heidi holds, Simone feels loosely suited to the task at hand.

"Heidi, why don't you go ahead and put your designs up on the corkboard."

Heidi makes a show of uncrossing her legs and standing slowly. Simone wonders if James asked her to do the pinning just so he could watch Heidi as she lifts her arms and one foot to get it all just right. Simone also wonders if Heidi struggles just a little too much to give him more time to appreciate her assets.

The whole thing makes Simone's stomach turn.

The smile Heidi gives James before she sits down embarrasses Simone. She turns her attention to what's on the wall instead. Thankfully, Simone doesn't have any emotional response to what she sees. The designs are textbook and look a lot like the line she helped James design last spring.

Simone turns to see what he thinks. Apparently, he is having the same thoughts. Simone cringes. She has a feeling for what might come next.

James spends the next five minutes asking Heidi questions about the minute details of her designs. His tone is sober, nearly nice, at times borderline encouraging. But Simone knows better. James is disappointed. His eyes are dull, and he hasn't even dropped his feet off his desk to stand up and get a closer look.

Heidi, on the other hand, seems to take time to fully register his disappointment. He is saying enough of the right things to keep her from crying or overtly offending her. Simone sucks in a shallow breath. It sucks to sit where Heidi is right now, and the more Ficklow says, the more Simone's sliver of empathy grows.

All altruism is cut to the quick when James stands up and takes the designs out of Simone's hands. Frankly unsure of what James will see in them, she waits and does her best to control the rising bile in her throat. It makes her nervous to have her work critiqued, especially in front of others. Restless, she sets her coffee down and stands up. To avoid threatening his authority, she leans against the wall and faces him.

For ages, Ficklow stands there with his weight on one leg and a hand across his mouth. Then he starts to talk, directing his comments to Heidi. Pointing out where Simone did what on which design. Mostly, his comments are to educate Heidi on what she should have done differently.

He is taking forever. Stars flood Simone's vision. She bends her knees. Her vision clears, she exhales. Simone loosens the knot at her throat. One action at a time brings her back into the room and the conversation James and Heidi are having.

"If you had brought this side slit up to mid-thigh, you would be able to remove this chunky panel here." James unpins Heidi's design and puts it right up against one of Simone's. Then he takes out a black marker and draws lines across both of their drawings to make sense of what he sees.

Simone risks a glance at Heidi.

Heidi is as white as a sheet under her goldenrod foundation, and whether that is from anger or embarrassment Simone isn't sure.

Before dismissing them, Ficklow addresses Simone. "Much better this time, Simone. We will move forward with your designs, given you make the corrections we just talked about and draw up a clean set for submission."

Inwardly, Simone groans. If Ficklow hadn't drawn in marker on her pencil sketches, she'd have had a head start.

Aurora and Willow are right.

Ficklow is a dick.

Meeting adjourned.

When Simone flings open the door to the ladies' room, Heidi is already at the mirror freshening up. Simone does her best not to let the pity she feels show, but she doesn't succeed. Heidi narrows her hazel eyes, admires her slim profile in the mirror, and shoots Simone a look that says it all.

That's when it hits her: Heidi lost and she is pissed. Simone won, and she didn't even know there was a battle. Moreover, Ficklow used her designs to teach Heidi signature elements of his style. In the moment, it made her want to gag, and yet it is *her* submission going to Fashion Bolder. *Her* designs that could walk the runway in Berlin. She is only making the most minor changes.

Simone sits down at her desk with her back to Heidi. Within a few hours, she has the drawings and entry ready to file. She doesn't put Heidi's name anywhere on the entry. She runs everything past James one last time and holds her breath while he reviews the details.

She should feel confident when he gives her the green light, but the possessive and clammy hand Ficklow rests on her shoulder as she hits "Submit" floods her with disease. It reminds Simone of every reason why she chooses not to live in a big town. Why she has avoided working at huge competitive fashion houses. She can't stand working with others, sharing ideas and credit. It gets messy and emotional and people aren't always honest.

More than ever Simone wants out.

Out of Ficklow's grip. On my own. My terms. My decisions. My designs. My business.

9

*E*arly the next evening Logan meets Simone at her place after work with a host of questions he'd like to ask her. Adam left him with a lot to think about, and Reggie gave him enough warning to curb his initial high. But there is one thing Logan is confident about. He knows he can do a lot to ease Simone's burden, at least with what she has hired him to do. The rest will take time.

He cruises down Simone's alley and props his bike under her window. Simone is outside, sitting in one of her porch chairs sipping coffee. Her eyes are closed, and her face is angled toward the sunset. She has on the same heavy cardigan, but today it hangs open over a pale-yellow shirtdress. A little cluster of sparkly stones hangs from a chain around her neck. Her legs are crossed, her feet bare, and the upper one swings slowly.

Despite the relaxed posture, Logan can tell something bothers her. There is a crease between her eyebrows and tension in her chin.

She opens her eyes when she hears him and says, "I'm so glad you are here."

That one line settles Logan in. To know she is happy he is here makes a huge difference after what he heard from Adam last night. He sits down in the chair beside her. "I'm happy to be here. It is a beautiful evening."

Simone hums. "I have a bit of an update." She speaks through closed eyes. Logan can see the corners of her mouth start to pull down. "Ballistic Bride decided to replace one of her bridesmaids. She had a cryptic way of saying they weren't seeing eye to eye on some important things, so she had to withdraw her invitation altogether." Simone swallows hard.

Logan just waits. It is clear Simone needs time to say what comes next.

"Unfortunately, this new bridesmaid dress is in addition to two other recent additions—that is three she's added to the order outside of the original ten commissioned. She has a new maid of honor. I imagine pulling in an outsider for this important role is causing quite a stir among the other bridesmaids. So now, instead of just two dresses to finish, and the garters, in time to ship this order, I have an additional dress to make. A focal point dress, no less."

Logan gently comments, "They must have had a very serious difference of opinion to make this kind of change."

Simone can only nod and say, "Weddings bring out the worst in people."

"Not a very common opinion—most would argue the opposite. That weddings bring out the best and love is everywhere."

"I know better." Simone opens her eyes and gets up. "I'm headed in for another cup of coffee. Need one?"

Logan stands, too. "Bad experience?"

"Left at the altar."

Impressed with how frank she is, Logan follows her inside and takes off his shoes at the door. When he turns around, Simone is standing there with a cup for him. He takes it and smiles. She smiles and tips her head back to look up at him.

Behind her, the last sunlight streams in through the front door. The garage is cool, and Simone is the picture of warmth. Logan curls both hands around his coffee mug and smells it.

After taking a sip he says, "And now, I can sit down and sew nearly four hundred garters from a place of sanity."

Simone laughs. "That's all it takes? I wish I were that easy." She blushes at the innuendo, and Logan prefers her cheeks this shade of pink. "The changing aspects of this order make me insane."

"Are the dresses hanging here all a part of it?" Logan looks through the dresses, being careful not to touch them too much and move them only by the hangers.

Simone nods. "I've been working on it for nearly three months now."

"Have you been taking other orders on as well?"

There is an impressive amount of work here, and Logan knows what it takes to generate an order like this. He asks a few more questions, casually, carefully, until he has a better understanding about how her business is generated mostly by online reviews or word of mouth.

"I've only accepted single-item orders since I picked up Ballistic Bride. So a handful of bridal gowns. I finished all of them ahead of this last stretch for Ballistic Bride. Something told me it wouldn't be a straight shot across the finish line on this one."

"What made you take the order in the first place?"

Logan watches her weigh how much to share.

"I want the credit for it, for every little bit of it. She has a huge social media following and is marrying into a big oil family. Both her and her photographer have agreed in writing to let me use the photographs from her wedding. I want images of my work on real people at a huge event. This is a huge wedding party, thirteen dresses total, every single one different and custom made. It is over the top, but elegant. I'm tired of staged photoshoots with just a handful of models and need something that will set my work apart, give me a big pop of exposure to ideal clients, and establish me as a reputable designer with a ton of experience under my belt."

Logan puts pieces together in his mind. "Does it bother you that I'm the one sewing the garters?"

Simone chews on the inside of her lip. "It bothers me that something this significant would be carelessly added to an order that is already twenty percent greater than it was at the start. Budgeting my time around this has been too much."

Logan puts a hand on her shoulder. "Does it bother you?"

"Yes."

Logan barely nods.

"But your work looks inseparable from mine on something this small."

It is a minor concession. Logan wants to hug her, but her arms are crossed over her chest. Instead, he tucks a lock of hair behind her ear and pinches her chin.

Simone briefly closes her eyes. He watches the pulse hammering in her throat until it calms, and wills his heart to do the same.

10

*S*imone is glad she relished every second of the time she spent with Logan, because Ficklow is in rare form when she walks into the backroom Friday morning. She can hear him raging at someone on the phone in his office. Heidi is already there, all crisp and clean in yet another pencil skirt. Simone wonders how she breathes with a waistline that high and tight, or how she manages to eat anything at lunch without busting at the seams. Normally the picture of cool, Heidi also appears peevish at Ficklow's agitated tone of voice.

Simone risks a trip to the coffeemaker and printer for a chance to overhear some detail of his conversation.

"What do you mean?" His voice raises in pitch, and the hair on the back of Simone's neck lifts.

At the same time, the printer whirs and the door to his office slams shut.

Sliding out of the printer is the month's expense report and accompanying bar graph. She can't help but see an odd number. Five figures headed out of the account and into another. Expenses that big are normally budgeted for at the start of the year, and usually pass through Simone's production department. She doesn't recognize the name of the recipient or the account number.

Something is going on.

She has the worst feeling.

The second Ficklow hangs up Simone turns around, bumping right into Heidi. She spills black coffee down the creamy silk of her blouse. Heidi yelps. Simone tries to mop up the mess with micro cocktail napkins. Heidi practically snarls at her and bats her hands away with impatience.

Ficklow steps out of his office. He can tell what happened without having to ask. Simone brushes tiny invisible spots of coffee off of her black smock dress.

He turns to Heidi. "Pull a blouse off the floor for today."

Simone is shocked. Ficklow never lets employees wear clothes off the floor. Samples, yes, on occasion, but never ready-to-wear off the floor.

Heidi lifts her nose at Simone when he offers and spins on her heel to find her size.

It takes all of Simone's reserve not to trip Heidi on her way to the restroom to change.

Ficklow snatches the printout from Simone's hands.

She points to the charge. "There's something odd on there—"

But James walks away from her. "You don't write all of the checks around here, Simone."

～

"Gemma?" Simone opens the screen door to Gemma's house. She feels hollow after this week of work, empty, drained, confused. She didn't want to go home, where she spends time with Logan, where she starts things and ends them creatively. Inside Gemma's, the smells of baked goods and cannabis flood her with memories; they are everywhere, but the house is empty.

It has changed a lot over the years. First Willow owned it, and when the time was right, she sold it to Gemma. All refinished hardwood, the main floor is centered around an open kitchen with an island in the middle. She and Gemma lived here once with Willow during college, and they spent countless nights drinking wine at the big table. Aurora spent a good deal of time here, too, sleeping on the couch, though she never officially moved in. Together, the four of them endured many storms, and along the way the house transformed around them into a beautiful and nurturing home.

It was the first property Willow handled as a new realtor, and the first house Gemma bought. In an aging part of town, the house spent a decade in disrepair while the previous owner, a widow, lived out her days in a nursing home. When Willow moved in, she did her best to salvage and reuse what she could when it came to hardware and solid wood. Then, she added her touch, and now that Gemma has lived here alone for years, the place feels like a sanctuary. It is easy for Simone to find peace and stillness here.

She cruises past the low couch and runs her hands across its velvet cushions. The wooden table must have been freshly oiled. Simone can smell lemon on her fingertips.

Wandering out the french doors to a covered patio, Simone finally finds Gemma tucked deep into her backyard. She is in the middle of her garden, barefoot, blonde curls hanging past her waist, and a skirt full of green beans.

Gemma turns to Simone and greets her with an enormous smile. It wilts immediately when she sees the shadows beneath Simone's eyes and the pull in her lips. Guilt floods Simone for crashing her friend's sunny afternoon. They meet at the edge of the garden.

Simone can hardly talk. She toes off her shoes and gathers

up her skirt. Gemma wraps an arm around her and walks her back into the heart of the garden. When they are both standing barefoot on the good earth, Simone takes a deep breath. Her chest is so tight. Gemma takes her hands in hers, and Simone tries again. Tears start to flood down her cheeks. She doesn't try to stop them.

Gemma holds her hands; they feel secure. The wet dirt sucks Simone's feet into the ground. When the sensation of fainting starts to come over her, Simone bends her knees and Gemma follows her into a squat.

"Let it go, Sim." Gemma's request is gentle but firm. "Get it all out. You've been keeping it in for nearly a week now."

Simone starts to really cry. The tall beans and corn and whatever else Gemma grows tower over her. She is protected, and there isn't anyone but Gemma to see her crumble. It gets all ugly and just when Simone is on the verge of disgusted for making such a mess of herself, Gemma hands her a dishtowel, damp from drying washed veggies.

It is huge and white and soft, and Simone wrecks it.

She does her best to wipe beneath her eyes and all, but Gemma stops her and just says, "Follow me."

Back inside, she gives Simone a fresh bath towel and a cool glass of water. "Drink this and take a long shower. Help yourself to the products. There should be labels on them."

Simone hugs Gemma. "I love you."

Gemma's bottom lip starts to quiver, and her eyes tear up. "I love you, too."

Before Simone starts balling all over again, she downs the glass of water and turns for the shower.

Under the hot spray, Simone cries. Between courses of homemade soaps, shampoos and scrubs, she finds the complacency of numb. In the span of this past week her circumstances at work have become very clear. First throwing up at brunch, then therapy, now this. Something has got to change.

Gemma knocks and passes her a set of sweats. Simone accepts them and puts them on. When she opens the door, Gemma stands there with a glass of wine in each hand. Beyond her, Simone smells food cooking. The void in her stomach growls loud enough for Gemma to laugh.

"I'm making a feast. Aurora and Willow will be here shortly."

Minutes later, the four of them are at the table curled up around wine and appetizers.

Willow pushes back her curls and digs a carrot into fresh hummus. Through a full mouth she asks Simone, "Why the long face?"

Simone turns away and takes a big sip of wine. She's no good with teasing and Willow is an expert.

Aurora faces her. In her bright green eyes, pale and clear, Simone sees compassion. It takes her off guard. Aurora is her soul-sister, single-child confidant. "Don't look at me like that."

"Like what?" Aurora's deadpan delivery tells Simone everything she needs to hear.

"Like you can't fathom why I'd be so upset over anything that could possibly be happening in my perfect life."

Aurora puts up both hands. "I'm looking at you like enough already. Do the thing that must be done."

"Go easy on her if you want dessert," Gemma warns before she sets down a roasted chicken surrounded by a colorful veggie medley from her garden.

"What is it? What 'the thing' that needs to be done?" Willow asks.

"I'm not telling." Aurora fills her plate.

Willow rolls her eyes. "Fine. What happened? Did Ficklow steal your lunch?"

Simone starts to push her plate away. Gemma places a gentle hand on her wrist. She reaches out to Willow on the other side, who immediately stops talking.

Simone watches Willow's fiery temper flare at being checked by Gemma. Her pale cheeks flame with embarrassment. "You're really upset," she says. "I'm sorry. What happened?"

Simone isn't even sure why she is upset. "It's such a muddle."

Aurora tells her to start at the beginning.

"Well, you know Ficklow hired Heidi." Simone tells everyone about walking in this morning and what happened at the design meeting. She also mentions the phone calls and the spreadsheet.

Aurora opens up toward her and straddles the bench. "Just to be clear: He chose your designs moving forward?"

Simone nods her head.

Willow adds, "And it is your designs he used to put Heidi in her place?"

Simone shrugs.

Gemma concludes, "He has such a sick way of giving you the nod. Passive-aggressive."

"Very. On the one hand, I'm so happy to have this job and pay my bills and—"

"Yadda yadda yadda." Aurora is impatient for Simone to get to the crux of the matter. "But?"

"But I can't stand the fact that my day-to-day happiness is wrapped up with this manipulative asshole."

Willow starts clapping. "Ficklow just graduated from dickhead to asshole."

"It's true. He is so cruel, whether he recognizes what he is doing or not. And I know we need more help. I'm sinking under the workload as it is, and without help we won't meet our deadlines and buyer expectations or production schedules. But pitting her against me like that right from the start was so self-destructive on his part."

Again, Aurora motions with her hand for Simone to get to it.

"I want to be on my own. I can't stand him. Heidi is turning out to be the classic fashion bitch—some wannabe model who missed the height requirement by an inch, so she had to get a job making fashion instead. Not an ally. Women in this business are ruthless."

Leaning forward, Aurora really looks at Simone. To Simone, this feels like some sort of test. No matter what, she can't break eye contact with Aurora; it's important. Finally, Aurora leans back.

"I've been thinking about what you said to me during therapy, about entering the contest under an alias."

Gemma and Willow ask what this is all about, so Aurora takes a minute to fill them in on the idea. "But Simone might be too chicken to take a risk like this."

Simone swallows wine down the wrong pipe. She tries, but can't seem to counter what Aurora says. It's the whole reason why she couldn't come up with a single thing last night. "That's true, too. I'm scared shitless to enter twice. If both entries make it, I'm screwed. If Ficklow found out I went behind his back and entered under false contact information, that would be grounds for him to fire me. Getting accepted would mean being in direct competition with him. Competing would mean being in two places at once, and if I'm found out I could disqualify both entries. Even if I could maintain an illusion of the alias until then, it would come out at the most critical moment. It would ruin my career if Ficklow has a hand in defaming me."

Gemma clears the table while Simone explains.

The moment Simone takes a bite of warm apple pie, Aurora drops her bomb.

"Use Logan's information. Build a brand around it and submit designs. Run the risk right up until the last minute."

"Aurora's right," Willow agrees. "You are running a risk if

you *don't* enter twice. Ficklow is the type of person to use your designs and then dump you right before the competition if it suits his personal interests best. If you don't enter on your own, there is a chance you might not get there at all."

"Cross the bridge of being in two places at once when you get to the competition. There are many opportunities for things to sort themselves out on the way there." Gemma's confirmation is all Simone needs to consider really doing this.

"But," she hesitates, "I'd have to convince Logan to do this. I don't think it will be difficult. But what if he wants to be a part of everything? I mean, really a part of everything."

Gemma confirms it. "You'd kind of need him to, if you have to represent your line and Ficklow's in person. I know it doesn't sit well with you to rely on someone like this." Gemma is dancing around the issue.

Simone says what everyone is already thinking out loud. "I'm scared he will bail at the last moment, leaving me at the altar, a sacrificial altar."

Aurora doesn't mince words. "If you are in the competition and he bails at the last moment, then you'll have to do what you should have been doing all along."

"What?"

"Oh, honey," Gemma says. "You'd have to stand up for yourself."

All Simone can do is look bewildered.

"Relax," Willow pets her. "That all happens tomorrow. Tonight is Blues Night."

11

Simone can tell hitting Gemma's vape pen while getting ready tonight was a mistake. There are already too many people at The Salt Lick. Willow and Aurora can handle this crush, but she can't stand here and wait while guys edge in on her personal space.

The weed hits her all at once. She wants to close her eyes while the sensation passes, but she's afraid she'll do something stupid like fall over. When she takes a deep breath, a familiar smell and a strong arm envelop her.

"Hey."

Logan?

Somehow Simone finds her voice. "Hi."

Logan tightens his hold around her shoulders and moves her away from the bar. "You good?"

Simone's only answer is to wrap her arm around his waist. "I'm great, just lightheaded at the moment."

He tucks her into a small booth. There is a low light above the table. On the other side sits a handsome but younger and much stockier version of Logan.

"I'm Logan's brother, Reggie." The smile he offers her is just as charming as Logan's. It immediately puts Simone at ease. She shakes his hand. Reggie's hands are like Logan's, broad palms and long fingers.

"And I'm Svere Benhaus." Simone shakes Svere's hand. It is cool and dry and his eyes are kind. He's good-looking, no doubt, all millennial cool with spacers, long hair and his short beard. He is polished in ways that don't matter as much to Simone, and her initial impression is they don't matter as much to Svere, either. He just can't help it, like Gemma. When she looks over at Logan, his rugged handsome face appeals to her all the more.

On this side of the bar the AC is blasting. Little to none makes its way to the dance floor, and on Blues Night, this table is just the retreat she'd normally appreciate.

Simone doesn't say much. She's getting used to the dynamic of Logan in a social environment with his friends. She can't believe she has only known him a week. He is familiar in the best way, safe and supportive.

I must be super stoned.

She knows this should feel weird, but sitting next to him, tucked into this tiny booth at his side, she is incredibly comfortable. His body shelters her from the crowd and her weed induced social paranoia fades. At times, while he's in the middle of small talk, his hand slips and his fingers brush her shoulder. She tries not to read too much into that.

Within moments, Willow and Aurora are at their table, too. All smiles and questions as they introduce themselves and hand Simone a glass of wine. Willow makes a point of smirking when she sees Simone with Logan's arm around her.

Simone can easily explain how it happened, but she is spared when their friend Nico sneaks up behind Willow and pinches her in her ribs. Willow's smile reaches her eyes when Nico gives her a hug. Over her shoulder, he winks at Simone. She wonders why neither of them will admit they want each other. Together, the two are fire and ice. Willow's hot looks and temper set against Nico's infinite cool.

Reggie and Svere slide out of the u-shaped booth to greet the girls and Nico and it doesn't surprise Simone to see they know each other. Nico is the best mechanic in Boldene and has owned Pearl's Garage for years now. Because of his business, Nico knows most of the town. What does surprise Simone is how Svere and Aurora greet each other like the most familiar strangers ever. Their eyes lock over a handshake that is too formal, and Aurora looks immediately irritated.

Willow tucks into the booth beside Simone. "Nico is such a cutie. Look at him with the hair and the pants."

Nico wears what he always wears: Dickies pants and a dress shirt tucked in with a belt, but tonight he's peeled back his mechanic's coveralls and polished his boots.

Simone laughs. Nico has always had old world class, but she remembers a time when his reputation wasn't as sterling as it is now, and auto repairs weren't the only commodity he sold out the back of his garage.

When Nico and Logan greet each other across the table with a handshake, Nico looks at him in a different way with Simone tucked into his side. She is sure of it and it makes her self-conscious. Simone is definitely an only child in so many ways, and over the years of knowing Nico, he has stepped in as an older brother to help keep her life on the rails whenever it has threatened to careen off course.

Willow draws her attention by pointing out Aurora leaning against the wall with Svere. "What's going on over there?" she wonders out loud.

Aurora stands defiant, arms crossed over her chest, drink in one hand, staring at the band. She is practically ignoring Svere. But he isn't having it. He steps in front, blocking her view.

"I can't tell what he's saying," Willow says.

Svere reaches out to touch Aurora's face. It is intimate and tender and Simone knows Aurora can't stand it.

Even Willow flinches when Aurora dodges and walks away. She stops at their table to put down her glass. Simone knows that's her goodbye. The girls watch Gemma stop her at the door. She glances back at Svere, who still stands there watching her.

With his hands in his pockets and dress shirt open a couple buttons, Svere is the picture of indifferent hotness. Simone reads right through his nonchalance and can see Aurora has offended him.

"Svere's not used to being turned down," Logan says to Simone, startling her.

Logan's face looks concerned, and different. The creases next to his mouth where his dimples pull in are accentuated even more by candlelight. She loves how his eyebrows are like dark wings above his clear, blue eyes. From the set of them it is obvious he cares about Svere.

Simone excuses herself and heads straight to the ladies. She feels good. The music and conversation have mollified her senses, and the nagging feeling that she should be working has subsided. She rinses her hands under cool water, and the woman staring back at her in the mirror is someone she hasn't seen in a very long time. This girl is someone Simone finds beautiful. She adds some lip gloss and appreciates the glow Logan's attention has given her cheeks. Gemma did her hair, and the normally drab bob she wears sits stacked in the back and framed around her face. It almost looks like she has cheekbones.

But by the time Simone gets back to the table, Logan is gone. She just stands there for a second, a little befuddled. The disappointment hits her like a surprise gone bad, and for the first time tonight she's considering ducking out the back door. All the buoyant bliss and belonging she felt in the restroom moments ago has fled her body. Svere and Reggie are talking, Willow and Nico are dancing, Aurora has bolted.

She's alone.

On the verge of feeling ridiculous, she clutches her tiny purse, and the beading cuts back into her skin. She closes her eyes on a silent plea, and then, in an instant, Logan is back with another round of drinks.

How simple.

She made it so complicated in her mind. Simone can't tell if she is her own best friend or worst enemy at times like this.

She smiles into Logan's eyes and accepts the drink. She slides back into the booth with Logan following. As the music gets a bit louder and the lights dim a little lower, Simone realizes sitting beside Logan gives her a new place to be. The music is soulful and soft. Her body sways, and when she leans into Logan, he leans back. The sensation nourishes her.

She needs this. This friendship or whatever it is with him is so easy. Eventually, Logan turns his body enough so she can lean into him and see the band better. She has to resist the temptation to reach up and thread her fingers through his.

Tonight Gemma dolled her up with sparkles and a dress shorter than usual. When Simone crosses her legs, and the skirt rises higher, it is hard to be bold and leave it there. To not get self-conscious and tug the hemline into submission. She feels Logan's gaze briefly drop down to her lap. And when the crowd thickens, she has to sit even closer to him and rest her forearm on his thigh. His leg tightens and then relaxes as if adjusting to the sensation of her being there.

It makes her breath catch, and deep down, she'd like to be pressed against every inch of him. Just pressure, sensation, an ease to the discomfort of life right now. Logan turns his head, and she thinks he smells her hair. When he kisses her temple, it is barely a press of his lips, but the feeling cruises right down her body and lands in just the right place. She barely looks to him, just enough to let him know she felt that and would like more.

Soon Gemma brings her another glass of wine. Mirth surrounds Simone. Willow, Nico, and Reggie are laughing, and even though he is distracted, Svere seems amused.

Simone finds Logan's reflection in her wineglass.

"It's hot sex for you tonight." Willow's breath is close in Simone's ear.

Simone's cheeks burn with heat at the thought of it. She turns to her friend. Willow's face is deceptively sweet. All heart shaped with pouty lips.

"Oh Willow, my long-time friend, why do you have to be so hard on me?" Simone brushes stray locks of red back from Willow's face and licks her lips. "You are so tall and Viking beautiful. A brave defender. But why are you fierce with me?"

Simone's words run together a little bit with the wine, her tongue thick. Their faces are very close. Ease fills her heart, when Willow's expression softens. Willow kisses her on the lips. Startling Simone, making her laugh.

"I love you, Sim. It's hard for me to watch you struggle when happiness can be so simple. I'm not saying it's easy." Willow looks over Simone's head at Logan. "But it can be simple, if you share it."

~

For the first time since meeting Simone Logan wonders if he's had her all wrong. Has she only been flirting with him to piss off Willow? Logan wants to ask Nico questions, but it is Willow's eyes he meets first. There is no challenge there, just mischief and a what looks like a dare. Reassured, Logan waits for Willow and Nico leave the table, then he asks Simone to dance.

The song is low and slow, and at first Simone doesn't

answer him. Grateful she has had just enough wine to skip a beat, Logan pulls her out of the booth and into his arms.

Even with her wearing four-inch heels, Simone is still a foot shorter than Logan. At first he just takes her in, this little bolt of beautiful power in a wispy dress. Logan wants to lift the hem and separate the layers of fabric, see what's hiding underneath. He folds her to him, wanting her closer. He can tell Simone is quite strong. He slides his hands up her spine and down her arms. They dance through three or four songs together, losing track of when one ends and the next begins.

When Simone has relaxed into him and let herself melt against his legs and torso, he tips her chin up. Pale color shines on her eyelids. It takes time for her to open them. Her dark eyebrows peak in an unspoken question. Logan drops his head and sees her eyes widen as he kisses her. Then her arms curl around his neck and her body presses against his.

Her response is the welcome he needed. Wrapping his arms around her, Logan slowly lifts her up, their faces meet. He can see faded circles around her eyes and a flush across her lips. Her eyes are smudged with mascara, making them look an even richer brown. There is a new trace of happiness there. A sparkle to his fairy, fey, this sprite. She smiles slow and tired. Damp curls lay against her forehead. The band covers Otis Redding and sings about weary women. Logan leans in and really kisses her with tenderness.

Gemma interrupts them with a tap on Simone's shoulder. "Hey, sweetness, you're givin' the band a view of your cakes."

Logan smiles against Simone's mouth, and she laughs. When it is just the two of them again, Logan whispers into her ear. "Let me take you home."

Simone pulls back, and for a second Logan thinks he's just moved too far too fast and lost her. She focuses on something over his shoulder, and he denies the temptation to hold her tighter or pull her closer. Instead, he swings her out, and when she rolls back into him, she is breathless but grinning. Keeping her close, he feels her heart beating against his belly. Finally, Simone is the one to pull him closer and give him the answer he most wanted to hear.

~

Simone sits close to Logan during the cab ride. If she loses contact with him, she starts to doubt what she's doing. Time passing haunts her like a grumpy relation, crushing her buzz, reminding her of some chore she's ignored. But Simone is sure she wants this. On the bench seat next to her Logan draws her closer. He is a magnet. His pull is strong. He still smells clean and the arm around her feels solid and warm. She doesn't care that they work together. He works for her.

You know that is such a joke.

She checks his expression for any second thoughts, but there aren't any. His profile is steady. He's holding her hand to his thigh and has eyes trained on the street ahead of them. It winds and turns up the canyon a bit from the hills around her house. He tells the cab driver to pull over; they've arrived. The Victorian stands very tall and proud in the center of a long block with acre lots. It's dark, but the gingerbread paint job charms Simone.

Nervousness returns when they don't walk in through the front door. She expected the building to have been broken down into units. But they walk along the side of the house to the back. Behind the house is a steel staircase leading to the roof.

When they get to the bottom of the steep and zigzagging stairs, Simone hesitates. She looks up; it appears to be quite high. Her heartbeat picks up. The metal mesh plays tricks with her depth perception. Logan puts one hand on her waist to steady her. That alone has her slightly off balance. Beneath her sweaty palm, the handrail is cold and sobering. She focuses on taking one step at a time. The press and pull of Logan's hand takes up every other bit of her awareness.

Once inside his home, she is delighted. There are a lot of windows, and the town of Boldene spreads out below them in a tiny grid pattern of quaint lights. The organization of it soothes Simone's nerves and her head is crystal clear.

"Would you like a whiskey?"

Simone shrugs her yes.

Logan spends a few minutes puttering, and soon Simone hears music pour out of unseen speakers. Her heart speeds up, knocking tiny thumps against her throat. Her hands form crisp folds in her dress, while smooth curves bend through the liquid music. Flushing with sudden warmth, she stirs as Logan comes back with a glass. Simone tosses back the amber drink. There is something about Logan that makes her want courage. While he fills his glass, she says, "Pour me one more short one, please."

~

Drunk is how Logan feels when he cannot resist Simone. They are dancing now in his living room. She is tender and slight, and the elegant length of her arms holds him tight like a thin belt around his waist. Warmth seeps through to his skin, and he slides his hands up her back, searching for more. Her shoulder blades remind him of tucked wings, delicate and loaded with potential. He shifts his feet to either side of hers.

Logan kisses the corner of one eye and rubs his lips against hers, pressing them gently.

"Look at me, Simone."

She opens her eyes. Embers flare, and their sepia depths warm.

He gathers her dress into a fist. "I have ideas about the scarves you wear," he says and kisses her fully.

He can feel Simone respond immediately. He's delighted when the sweep of his tongue makes her part her lips and hum. She pulls him to her, curling his body to her so that more of hers makes contact with his. A warmth grows low in his belly.

Logan tips her head back and places wet kisses down her throat, reaching low to grab the hem of her dress and pull the fabric up. He slides his hand against the cool skin on her leg. She bends her knee, and he takes the invitation to reach higher curling along the inside edge of her thigh.

"I want this," she says and clasps his wrists.

He kisses her again and bends down to pick her up.

She loops her arms around his neck and wraps her legs around his waist. When his hands circle back to her hips and the warmth between them, she rocks into him and he tightens his hold.

Logan moves without hesitation, taking her to the bed. Simone sinks into the down and looks at him.

He holds the back of her knees and pulls her body to the edge. He kneels down and slides his hands up her torso, lifting her dress as he goes. He rumbles words loud enough only for him to hear then bows his head to kiss through the slip of fabric at the center of her warmth.

～

Surrounded by Logan, Simone doesn't feel how cool the night has become. He encompasses her, and surprisingly enough, she finds it easy to let that happen. When his hands squeeze her a little too hard, she feels the pattern of his fingertips make an impression, and it pleases her. She knows he is asking her to take this further.

She opens her eyes.

He looks down at her, the question resonating in the clear blue of his steady gaze. His face has a new expression. It is very serious, focused, no trace of quiet amusement in his deep dimples. This is the look of a man intent on knowing her.

Simone blushes and can feel the heat of it spread up her chest and throat to her cheeks.

Logan smiles just a little and rises up to takes his clothes off.

Suddenly, Simone is impatient. She tucks her hands under her thighs so she doesn't do something embarrassing. He is built well, with a dark streak of hair below his navel. He looks like a man who moves more than enough to be balanced and capable but not bound to the gym. She shivers, and Logan is back, pushing his way to crouch between her knees.

He holds her head and kisses her until she can't think. He presses her back into the bed, and his hands and mouth bring heat to the surface of her skin. He licks the freckle by her belly button and then Simone loses all track of the time, her worries, her fears, her doubts.

She falls asleep wrapped up in him, incapable of feeling the difference between her body and his, incapable of finding the edge of where she ends and he begins.

~

The moon wakes Simone up, a steady beam flooding her eyes. When she realizes where she is, and how Logan's whole apartment is dark but for the moon's spotlight on the bed, she feels naked and on center stage. She sits up, drawing the sheet to her, and looks more closely at the apartment around her. It is a blend of antiques and functional pieces of furniture. In the dark, she can see Logan is tidy, but not compulsive. Examining her surroundings reminds her of where she is and what she has just done.

Blurred the edges of business and pleasure. Serious business, serious pleasure.

Logan sleeps soundly beside her.

Then it hits her. Midnight is the deadline for Fashion Bolder entries.

Rising like bile in her throat, anxiety floods her system. The mix of alcohol and panic lands her on the bathroom floor. She has no idea how long she is there, but the next thing she knows, Logan is picking her up.

But she doesn't want to get up; she wants to lie down on the cold tile floor until this whole thing is over.

"Simone, come here." Logan pulls her into his lap, and she lets him. "What's wrong?"

Simone doesn't want him to think she regrets sleeping with him. Through the haze of her discomfort that point feels very important.

"Nothing." She pretends to get up.

"Feels like something."

Simone takes a deep breath, and while the threat of vomit still swims below the surface, she slowly explains about the competition and how she wants to enter it on her own, but that it will likely constitute a contract violation, jeopardize both entries, and be physically impossible because of the whole thing about being two people in one place if both entries make it to the finals. It is exhausting to explain again, let alone accomplish.

Logan leans against his bathtub connecting the dots. "You want to use my contact information to enter the contest on your own? Why not use one of your girlfriends' information?"

Simone starts to feel like this might not happen. Like it is too much to ask. "This is a small enough town. My boss, James Ficklow, knows my friends."

Because she can't stand feeling left behind, disappointed, or dismissed, Simone gets in front of what she sees as inevitable. "Never mind. It's too much to ask. We don't know each other that well." She gets up and on shaky legs walks out of the bathroom.

Logan stops her from picking up her dress and hands her his robe instead. "You are cold."

She can read between the lines. "I didn't mean that. I'm sorry." Logan wraps her in his oversized, super-lush robe. It is a cocoon of his smell. "I'd understand if you don't want to do this."

Logan slides his hands up the lapels, gathering them together right at the place above her heart. The weight of them grounds her. She lets her head fall back, remembering the feeling of him deep inside her.

Please, help me.

The thought takes her off guard and puts her desire in perspective. She needs his help. In need is an uncomfortable place for Simone to be.

"Breathe." Logan issues the soft command, and Simone lets out the breath she's been holding in.

Logan cradles her face in his hands. "I'm happy to help and will do my best to make things easier for you."

It sounds like his offer extends beyond the scope of this project, and while that freaks her out a little bit, she actually trusts Logan. He is capable. Accomplished. A gentle giant. And if she turns her head, she can rest it on his chest and hear his heart beating.

"Thank you."

He kisses the top of her head. "How long do we have?"

"Until midnight."

His chest rumbles on a low laugh. "We have less than an hour. You *are* exciting."

12

_L_ogan gets Simone set up in the bed with a drawing pad before he grabs his computer. "I'm assuming you need to come up with another brand—your boss knows about your private label, right?"

Simone nods. "I use my last name, so it's just _Bonhomme_. We could do the same here. You have a great last name."

The man in Logan roars when Simone says that.

"What if, eventually, after you have won the competition, you wrap this label in under _Bonhomme_?"

"That would really be ideal. I've spent so much time getting that work exposure, and I'm on the verge of that good marketing material."

"Let's optimize all of it. What if we call this label _B. Clearwater_ and later you drop the Clearwater?"

"Sure." The whole time they are discussing names, Simone is sketching fluidly. Within fifteen minutes she hands him the drawings. "I can't believe it all just flowed out of me. I've been trying for weeks to pull these ideas together."

Her eyes are shining, and a big smile opens up her face.

It makes Logan's heart ache.

Lightly drawn on coarse paper are one bridal gown and three bridesmaid dresses. The bridal gown is sketched from three angles, the front, back, and a three-quarter view. It is a simple, long and flowing lace sheath. The tucked bodice has a V neckline with thin straps covered in wild floral lace. The long skirt has two layers, and they seem to float around the legs. A waist-length veil covers the open back in a diaphanous film. It is secured over the hair and at the brow line with a floral head-piece reminiscent of a flapper headband.

Each bridesmaid dress is different, yet they are united by the texture of georgette and silk. The color palette is neutral, very pale pinks, dusty blues, sage greens, and antique creams. The drape of all the dresses is nearly casual, reminiscent of 1920s sleeveless gowns with dropped waists, beading and multiple layers. Two of the three dresses end at the knee or above, the third hits just below. Many different body types could wear these looks well—and with comfort and ease.

"I can see some of the bits you used in the order for Ballistic Bride showing themselves here." Logan is careful with the drawings and arranges them on the wood floor under a good lamp. He takes photographs of each one and transfers them to his computer. Within just a few minutes, he has filled out the entry form with his contact details and attaches the sketches.

Simone is wrapped up and worrying the sheet beside him.

"You okay? Are we missing anything? You look nervous."

Simone looks at him. The moment of victory she just had at channeling the designs is nowhere to be seen. "I am nervous. There are details we haven't discussed. I need to be clear: this is my entry. You are part of it in name and numbers only. When this is over I own all the designs, the work, everything gets cred-ited to *Bonhomme*. Right?"

"Right. And when you win, the funds will all be deposited into your account. Simone," Logan says and sets aside the computer. He takes her hand in his. "This is your entry. I'm here for support, but this is all you. Maybe if things go well, you'll take me with you to Berlin." He winks.

Simone scoffs, but also starts to cry a little bit. He can see a war happening beneath the surface of her features. She is reining in her emotions, but Logan can't tell if everything is good.

"Are these happy tears?"

Simone closes her eyes, and a cache of saltwater spills down her cheeks. He wipes them away with his thumbs and kisses her. "Trust you can handle the outcome either way. I understand what you are doing makes you uncomfortable. It is bending the rules. Is the reward for getting in on your own greater than the risk of disqualification and losing your job?"

"I think so. I want it to be. I think it has to be. This is my chance. I just have to pray it works itself out before I get found out. Money is a thing, so I don't want to lose my job and would prefer to quit only if I have something else lined up. This could ruin my professional reputation in Boldene if it goes bad. But, it could go bad anyway because I think my boss might be cheating to win. If I don't take this chance now, I'll have to wait another year and hope the competition happens again."

Logan has a whole host of ways around Simone having to wait another year for a chance at Berlin. But, instead of reassuring her of that, he says, "I don't want to rush you, but it is time to make a decision. We have less than three minutes to send this off."

"Fuck!" Simone laughs in a watery way and sniffs back her tears. She takes a deep breath with closed eyes then opens them. She smiles again and says, "Okay, GO!"

Logan hits "Send," and the telltale *swish* is the last thing he hears before he closes the laptop and pulls the sheets over their naked bodies. It takes him a while, but Logan rubs and kneads every nook and cranny on Simone's lovely body to the point where no trace of anxiety or doubt remains. Then he curls her into him and listens as she falls asleep.

It is Logan who stays awake thinking, staring at the moonlight cascading over the bed. Countless minutes pass as he takes in the details of Simone and the surprise that is her, here with him now. And, the miracle that is the two of them working together on more. However long that might last.

Finally, he falls asleep, dreaming of Simone in that dress and veil.

13

$\mathcal{I}$t isn't until after noon the following morning that Logan drops Simone off at her apartment. He kisses her at the front door, and she watches him walk around the back to his car. Even as he walks away, she can feel the enchantment and strength of him leaving her. Once inside, she is faced with the aftereffects of one of the hardest weeks of her life.

The wreckage is everywhere.

She leans against the door, and the lock clicks loudly behind her. Simone's body is floating on a high of countless hours of the best sex of her life. It aches in deeply satisfying ways. At the same time, her mind is sabotaging that happiness and taking a nosedive into a cesspool of guilt and shame. If last night were like any other Blues Night, she would have gone out, danced her ass off, and landed back in this apartment just buzzed and humming enough to clean it like a whirlwind and wake up today ready to work on *her* stuff.

But, oh, dear God.

Everything has changed. There is evidence of Logan in all the corners of her space: his machine sits next to hers, their dirty dishes stacked in the sink. She hides her face in her arms and smells him on her skin. In the span of one long evening, she has managed to compromise her heart, her creative independence, and practically form a professional partnership.

Simone flashes back to the summer following her graduation from college. She's in a packed church, dressed in a wedding gown she made herself. There is chaos and disarray because her groom is nowhere to be found. Her friends do their best to help her manage, but there is nothing anyone can say.

It was the singular most embarrassing moment of her life. And the fact that she felt embarrassed above all other possible emotions that day told her she had said yes to partnership with the wrong person.

The feeling etched itself in her memory, and since then, Simone has resisted any desire to relive the moment, even if it were to have an alternate ending. At all costs she wants to avoid ever being ditched again at the last minute, ever having to excuse the behavior of others to those she loves.

This is as close as she has gotten since then to taking such a big risk. Simone groans. The booze last night gave her enough courage to let her guard down, let his warmth inside, let him ignite her. If she hadn't run into him, danced and slept with him, then confessed her desire to use him for his name and contact information, then...

Then she'd be totally up *Schitt's Creek* without a paddle in Ficklow's boat.

And that would truly suck.

Simone has a hard time acknowledging Logan rescued her. He picked her up off the floor and gave her permission to "do the thing." As Aurora would say. Left her with no reason not to go for her dream, not to at least try and see if her designs can make it into the competition without Ficklow's name attached.

It is all a muddle in her mind.

Simone gets up off the floor and clears a space at the front window. She lights a candle and some incense. She sits back down on a cushion, closes her eyes, and does her best to breathe deeply, steadily, focusing on anything but the lingering hangover and Logan. She very slowly walks her mind to stillness so she can see what she most needs to see and experience.

It takes time. She is out of practice.

And, she is distracted with nagging thoughts. It is never just going to be business as usual with Logan, and it is never going to just be sex, either. Instead of the clear and singular path to success she had envisioned, Simone must now see Logan standing with her.

She returns to the candle, steady in spite of its wavering flame. She closes her eyes, willing herself to see the flame on the back of her eyelids. Soon the flame is eclipsed. All she can see is Logan standing behind her, hands on her shoulders, a guardian at the ready. She tries again to see him at her side, a partner on her path for a short time only. But it doesn't come. He refuses to share the light.

Well. Now. I'm...

To her own astonishment, against his frame Simone shines bright and bold. So bright her light dissolves the edges of her body and she embodies the flame and Logan becomes the container, clearly discernible.

Simone fights the urge to break her meditation and stand up. Doubt invades her. Should she be concerned about this? It looked like she just dissolved her identity into the container Logan created. In no way does she want to lose herself.

Remember what you have created. It's just for show. B. Clearwater is just a facade. Just words on paper.

I captain this ship.

Doubt, you're a liar.

Simone can tell those thoughts are her ego rearing its ugly head. Taunting her with the lie that alone her life is controllable, that she can avoid hurt and pain if she doesn't let anyone close enough to understand her. Rationally she knows avoiding hurt and pain are impossible.

Simone's eyes feel gritty, and when she opens them, they won't focus right away. Her heart hurts. She understands why Logan is in her life. He is the container, but truthfully there is nothing for him to contain. She has a sneaking suspicion that his energy is what will free her light to shine; it will offer her protection, like a lantern to an open flame. It will not stifle her or suffocate her, or temper her brilliance.

It takes a long time for her to want to get up and move and break the spell of that vision, that truth. She holds it at bay. Logan's presence surrounds her and she can feel him inside her. It thrills her and scares her at the same time. She is frightened by the vulnerability inherent in the exposure she seeks, both with Logan and in her career. It is unavoidable, but Simone believes it is controllable.

She brings these visions down to earth by cleaning and scrubbing every last surface in her apartment and compartmentalizing and containing Logan's influence on her physical space.

14

*M*onday is one of those classic gray days in Boldene. Verdant moss grows on the sidewalk and hangs from green trees, and all that energy is socked in by a thick layer of clouds. These green-box, gray-lid days never deterred Logan's mood, and today is no exception.

Reggie sits down on his front stoop next to him. It's a narrow brownstone type of building stacked against three others. Reggie sinks his head into his hands and pushes his hair back.

Logan asks, "Tough day trading options?"

"I don't want to talk about it. The learning curve there is so steep!"

Logan laughs. Reggie's ability to teach himself nearly anything impresses him. Logan hands him a meatball sandwich. It's a peace offering of sorts. Logan wants to ask Reggie about a taboo topic. He's slightly hesitant, but it's a must. He starts off with a simple declaration.

"Simone wrestles with anxiety."

Reggie knows a lot about panic and anxiety. When their

mom first left, it was hard for Reggie to sleep at night, and panic attacks would wake him up.

"The same thing happened last night that used to happen with you."

Reggie mops red sauce off his mouth and swallows. "That's tough."

They sit in silence finishing sandwiches. Logan doesn't want to rush Reggie, but he also doesn't want his brother imagining the worst.

Reggie stuffs the last bite into his mouth and chews. Midway through he says, "Begin at the end."

"When we left The Salt Lick?"

"Yeah—to go lick each other's parts. Duh."

Logan winces because that sounded crude, and there is nothing crude about Simone. "It's not like that." He collects their garbage, putting it all back into the sack lunch came in. As they walk to Nico's garage, he describes everything about his time with Simone. Everything but the sex.

He talks straight through until he is done explaining their entry into the Fashion Bolder competition.

Reggie stops walking and looks up at the sky. "Oh no."

"What?" Logan asks.

"This is bad."

Logan starts walking again. "It's not bad." He's pissed enough to spit. "I didn't do any of it *for* her. None of it was *my* idea. I am only helping her go for her dream."

"Look, bro, I love you. I know you really want the best for everyone. I also know you have a tendency to think you know what the best is for everyone until proven otherwise. Be sensitive here. I heard you concocting ideas in your mind at poker. Are you sure none of this was you?"

"She hates her boss, wants to quit her job, and needs a break big enough that her business will support her in earnest.

All I've done is let her use my name, address, and phone number as tools to enter."

Reggie gives Logan a one-arm hug and says, "Forgive me. I feel like I need to protect you. No offense, but you suck at this game and it's not your fault. It's how you are wired. You've always been the one to step in and rescue anyone you see struggling, including me. I'm grateful, but also that backfires on you with women. They are different birds."

"This isn't going to be another Angie. I can smell infidelity tendencies from leagues away."

"And what about the rebound you helped to start a chain of yoga studios?"

Logan rolls his eyes at that debacle. It took nearly three years to iron out the legalities of his investment when the romance went bad. "You have a good point there, but I'm not financially staking Simone. I'm working out a plan around that, so just in case the competition doesn't work out she has another option, but I won't be the one to stake her personally."

"What's your angle, then?"

Logan glances sideways at Reggie. "That sounded cynical. There is no angle. This isn't a business deal."

"It sounds like a business deal to me. You've spent more time talking about what you did on paper last night than what you did between the sheets."

"That's because talking poetry would put you even more on guard."

Reggie stops walking. "Look, Logan. She's beautiful, no doubt. And weirdly enough you two fit together like a giant and his nymph, but take a breath. Even if it is just for her sake. Don't do anything, tread water for a little bit."

Logan takes Reggie by the elbow and drags him forward.

"Easy, Buddha. Treading water is still doing something."

Reggie chews that thought. Before he can say more, they are at Pearl's Garage, and Nico walks out to greet them.

"My good man," Logan says. "How's my Caddie?"

Nico wipes the grease off his hands and shakes Logan's.

"Humming like bumblebee."

Together, they look at the clean engine. Logan has a basic idea of how an engine should go together, but Nico understands how to assemble an engine so it sings. He has done more than take this rusty tub of parts and make it function again. He's returned it to its natural beauty. The engine sounds almost brand new, and while the car is in desperate need of a paint job and body work, she is beautiful to Logan from the inside out.

When they come out from under the hood, it surprises Logan to see Reggie talking with a girl. She's about his height, but smaller, a fraction of his weight, and dressed entirely in black from head to toe in way too many oversized layers. She is beautiful, with porcelain skin and done-up jet-black hair. He can also see piercings and tattoos in many places. She seems more preoccupied studying cracks in the cement than participating in conversation with Reggie.

Reggie, however, is oblivious to her disinterest. He's leaned against the doorjamb across from her, laying on the charm.

"Monica," Nico says, interrupting them. "This is Reggie, and his brother, Logan. Logan owns the Cadillac."

Monica nods and turns around. Less than a minute later, she hands Logan a clipboard with his paperwork, and takes his payment. Nico talks to her in Russian the entire time, and it is clear that what he says pisses her off. She offers Logan his receipt and glares at Reggie, waving him out of the way when she shuts the office door.

Reggie's eyebrows go up, and he smiles. "Nico, how long has she been here?"

Nico shakes his head at Reggie. "Off limits."

"Come on."

"She's my cousin. She's off limits." Nico grabs the Caddie's keys off a peg board above his tool bench.

"Why?"

"She's only here for a little while."

"But I can still show her around. She needs friends, right?"

Logan wants to make fun of the way Reggie follows Nico around the garage, seeking permission.

Nico stops walking and says, "She needs to heal and get well."

Reggie presses further until Nico finally caves and out of impatience answers him. He talks in a whisper and looks at the door to the office the whole time. "We grew up in the same village in Russia. Our families were very close, I was best friends with her twin brothers. They died a few years ago in a car crash. All of them were in the car together. She's the only one who survived, and she feels guilty about it. We both feel guilty about it, but it is in the past and there was nothing we could have done to change it." He talks in a whisper and looks at the door to the office the whole time. Logan can tell Nico feels the loss still and is very protective of Monica.

Reggie and Logan exchange a glance. Reggie says, "All right. I won't push. But, Nico, remember I'm a good guy."

Nico claps him on the shoulder. "I know. It's not about that. It's about her being okay with herself first. She's not in a good place with that yet."

Nico swings the hands on the "out to lunch sign" to read "back in twenty minutes." He shouts through the office door to Monica. "I'm closing the door to the shop for a bit so we can take Logan's car for a quick spin."

Logan catches the keys and slides into the driver's seat. Everything about this car suits him: the space he has between his knees and the dash and the bench seat in front with plenty of room across the car; the skinny steering wheel and humble horn; the analogue radio and the rag top.

The thrill this treat gives him reminds him of Simone, and he can't wait to take her for a ride.

Nico opens the back door for Reggie and then sits shotgun to walk Logan through the little touchy places on the car's transmission.

They cruise up and down the hills on the east part of town so Logan can get the hang of how things should sound.

Nico breaks a long comfortable silence down the only straightaway stretch.

"What's up with you and Simone?"

In the rearview mirror Reggie tosses up his hands. "Thank you."

Logan glances at Nico. "I noticed you two know each other. How does everyone in this town know Simone but me?"

"And me." Reggie pointedly looks at Logan in the mirror. "Tell us Nico. From what Adam Bear says, she isn't into having a boyfriend."

Nico clears his throat and turns his attention back to the road. "Tight turns coming up, might want to slow down until you get a feel for how to handle the curves."

Logan drives the automobile through the canyon, appreciating the direct connection his hands have with each of the moving parts. He likes how this car can be fixed with a screwdriver and a wrench. There isn't any computer or artificial intelligence to get in the way of making this machine purr. He knows Nico was alluding to Simone when he talked about slowing down to handle curves. This car and Simone are very much alike. Both are beautiful, classic, graceful; they just need a little tender loving care.

"I'm not out for a joyride with Simone." Logan downshifts into a turn and then right when they've come around the crux, he hits the gas and brings the luxury boat of a car through the turn on an upshift without losing any speed.

"I'm not Simone's brother," Nico begins and takes out a cigarette. He motions to Logan, asking his permission to smoke. Logan is sure hundreds of butts have been scrubbed out in the dash ashtray over the course of this car's life. He's willing to add to the stale smell of smoke in order to hear what Nico has to say about Simone. "I'm not even her cousin, for that matter. But I've known her for a long time. I met her when she moved to town for her first year of college. She came into my shop and asked for a paper bag, because there was a dead bird out front. I could tell she was heartbroken but didn't want to show it."

He takes time to light and then exhale out the window. "I can still see that bird. He was so beautiful, almost floating, blue and green and buoyant in a gutter full of still water. With the reflection of the sky, and the vivid color of his markings. I don't think I can ever forget how lovely, and sad, and mysterious he was. This gorgeous, foreign thing, some creature I had only seen from afar in motion or perched high on a branch. It was tragic, I felt that profoundly, and at the same time it felt like a gift. It felt like some gap had opened in the fabric of creation and I could see a lonely, still bird up close."

Nico looks out his window at the last field before town. Logan and Reggie are silent, both know it is better to let the normally tacit Nico finish if he's on a roll.

"Adam's right. Simone had a boyfriend all through college and he asked her to marry him. She planned the whole thing, made her own dress and one for each of her girls. Then that asshole left her, literally, standing at the altar, and flew off on the honeymoon by himself. She handled that day and its aftermath with incredible maturity. Every one of us was already there, the church was decked out, and the caterers were set up. We all took food home and the rest went to the shelter. Simone did her best to hide her disappointment and embarrassment. She piled plates full of food for the homeless in her dress. By the time she was done, there were splashes, drips, and stains all over it. I thought she might have done it for spite, but I think she was beyond even thinking about it. Shock and incredulity took over and sent her into practical mode. She's been on her own ever since. Willow says she buried the whole thing so deep it can't be excavated. No one is allowed to even mention his name. He never came back to Boldene."

"No wonder."

Nico doesn't respond, and Logan appreciates that. He needs time to think. The more information he gets about what makes Simone the way she is, the more it all makes sense, and the more he understands some of her choices. A true partner might be just the thing she doesn't know she needs. He glances in the rearview mirror, and Reggie meets his gaze. Logan reminds him not to get ahead of himself.

Right now, they have two projects together. First, finish Ballistic Bride. Then, focus on winning Fashion Bolder. Along the way, Simone needs a solid dose of old-fashioned romance.

Reggie interrupts his scheming. "Based on everything that has been said, my recommendation is to take a giant step back and give this woman some breathing room."

"Let her set the pace?"

Logan can feel Nico's eyes on him, but it is Reggie who presses harder. "If you don't she might freak out and cut you off."

Suddenly, there isn't enough space in the cab of the car. "I'm the lynchpin," Logan says. "The contest has my information; I have to show up for the meetings. Simone and I have discussed the details, and even if she tried to run, Boldene is a small town. Wherever she landed, she'd find me waiting for her. This feels like a crossroads moment for her, and for me, too. I didn't push for anything last night. It was as though she'd already thought the whole thing through and only needed to ask me if it was okay. I've spent a week getting to know her well. I'm up for seeing this through, wherever it goes. It's all part of the plan."

Reggie rolls his eyes. Logan doesn't even have to look at him to know he does it. He can practically hear it.

He cranks down the window for the rest of the drive back to

the garage. The fresh air emboldens him. "Our lives are written in the stars, little brother. Whenever it feels right, whenever light aligns, we are living our best life. Spending time with Simone, helping her with this, feels right. I have no expectations, nothing at stake but my time and emotions. Both I'm willing to invest."

15

Simone calls Logan just before noon on Monday.

"Ficklow's entry got in," she says, rushing the words together in nervousness the second he says, "Hey."

"Congratulations!" Logan's enthusiasm is genuine, and Simone can feel his smile through the phone. She wishes she didn't suspect the spot to be bought.

Then it hits her and she laughs because it *is* good news. Bought spot or not, she has designs in the running for Berlin! She hears his chuckle and closes her eyes. It sounds like the feel of his hands on her waist, pulling her to him.

Right away she's distracted by memories and imaginings, and in the midst of her thoughts, Logan asks her if she knows anything about twin flames or doppelgängers or parallel dimensions. Maybe quantum physics, string theory, time travel, or cloning?

At first, his questions knock her off guard; she can't follow his tack. But then, Simone starts to get the bigger picture.

"Tell it to me straight." She stands still in the middle of the pedestrian mall, tourists walking past, parting to divide and walk around her.

"*B. Clearwater* also got admitted. Simone, you have two sets of designs in the running."

Logan's voice is so pure, so quiet, so confident on the other line.

Simone curls up into a tiny ball and jumps. She did it! She squeals, and it draws too much attention. She feels her skin turn red from her throat up.

She's out of breath. Her heart is racing.

She's been admitted twice.

"How does it feel," he asks, "knowing no one called in a favor for your spot?"

Simone warms because Logan gets her. "It feels fantastic."

"Your work is good according to people who know, remember that."

Simone allows the victory to sink in for a moment before the practicalities start to sink her ship. She nearly passes out thinking about the workload facing her. The magnitude of two submissions on top of the regular production aspect of her job, plus Ballistic Bride.

"How am I going to do this?"

"Simone?" Logan sounds like he's at the bottom of a well.

She tries to slow her breathing down; her vision begins to fade.

Logan calls out to her again.

She puts the phone back up to her ear.

"Let it go. Let all the air out," he says. "Now, breathe in super slow. Just stand still. All right now, Simone. Baby, talk to me."

His tender endearment brings her back into her body.

Logan is the one to take a deep breath now. "Have you told Ficklow yet?"

Simone can't believe she hadn't thought to tell him first! "I'm headed to his office right now." She faces the storefront window.

Heidi and Ficklow are standing shoulder to shoulder looking out at her. She feels like she's been caught red-handed stealing or something. "Fuck. He's staring at me through the window."

Logan laughs. "Imagine I've just kissed your nose. Now, I'm following the line that begins at the bow of your lips right down the middle of your body. Later, I'm going to kiss you places that make you growl."

Simone blushes and turns away from the window. She hides her expression behind the dark curtain of her hair. "Logan..."

"There. Now you can go back inside and tell your boss you just got all aflutter about the new guy you're seeing. Then I want you to sit down to your desk, open your email, and flip out all over again because your submission got him into the competition."

"Right." She squares her shoulders and clears her throat.

"Then wrap up your day at work and let me take you out tonight. Or rather, let me pick you up. It is Reggie's birthday and I'm fixing him his favorite meal."

Simone's first impulse is to decline. Her default answer is always work before play, and since there is always work to be done she rarely goes out to play. But when she takes mental stock of where they are with Ballistic Bride's order, it is clear they are ahead of target for mailing on time this week. The orientation meeting for Fashion Bolder is the day after tomorrow. While there is still so much to be done to get ready for the competition just three weeks away, nothing can happen until they attend the first meeting and get the details. Left with no excuses, Simone gets to choose what she wants this time, and a homecooked meal sounds like just the thing.

Plus, she owes Logan.

I'm doing it. We are doing it.

"That sounds lovely," she replies.

Again, Logan assures her tonight is a celebratory evening of fun.

Simone's heart skips at the thought of it. She wants to know more about him, about the way he makes everything feel better. She wants to be the person she is when she is with him.

Knowing dinner is less than a few hours away gives her the fortitude she needs for the charade ahead.

$\sim$

It took longer to leave work than she'd expected. Instead of the tension-melting shower she'd envisioned, Simone settles for a quick rinse of everything but her hair and emerges from a three-minute shower pink and smelling like Gemma's grapefruit and peppermint scrub. She slips a dress over her head, stacks her bob again in the back, and uses a bit of mascara. A touch of sparkle here and there and in her jewelry and Simone is done. She pulls the door to her garage closed and locks it before she pockets the key.

Logan is waiting for her in one of the chairs on the porch. When she turns to him, her breath catches. He surprised her.

"I could hear you showering, so I gave you some privacy." Logan's face is open and warm. There is a hint of five o'clock shadow on his cheeks and a bit of play in the cock of his hat.

Butterflies start very low and slow in her belly as she sees herself through his eyes. Backlit by the low sun, Simone imagines her dress is translucent. There are layers and layers of fabric to it, but they are all as light as can be. The creamy muslin cascades to just past her knees, and the bodice hugs her chest closely. Tiny pin tucks ascend into straps, which cross in the back. At the last second, she added pink lipstick and two tiny bobby pins to pull one side of her hair back from her face, leaving the rest of it to fall forward. When she sees his expression, Simone wonders if it is too much for the occasion.

A blush floods her cheeks. Thankfully, before she becomes too self-conscious, Logan stands and reaches for her. Drawing her close, he kisses her and whispers, "You are incredibly beautiful."

Her confidence floats free of worry's weight.

Drawing back from her just a bit, Logan asks with skepticism, "Can you ride a bike in your dress?"

Simone smiles, a little shy, a little timid. She dialed it up for tonight and got noticed for it. It is fun to reward herself and Logan this way. It feels fresh and flirty and fucking racy. "Of course."

Lacing his fingers through hers, Logan leads her to the side of her garage where their bikes are parked. Simone lays her big brown leather tote bag and light-blue cardigan in the basket up front and follows Logan into the alley.

It is a gorgeous evening, still very warm, and everything looks spring clean and brand new. For about fifteen minutes, they weave their way across town, and Simone is content to simply follow his lead. The smell of blooming linden trees saturates the air in places. Everything that has been growing green seems to be unfurling and getting denser, lusher. It is the best kind of cozy to Simone.

Rounding a quiet corner, Logan rides his bike up to Reggie's brownstone. Almost on the opposite side of town from Simone's apartment, Reggie's sits on the small rise of a foothill with a view of Boldene. By this late in the day, his place has already been in the shadows for a bit. The sun is sinking lower in the sky, and it is full of drama. Streaks of orange and pink streak through the small city. Simone soaks it in, shivering as her body cools from the bike ride. She breathes in the fresh air, the smell of new life and all things green. It makes her happy.

Turning to follow Logan, she takes his hand, and together they walk through the open door.

Reggie is standing in front of the refrigerator. Arm draped

over the door, his body bent into empty shelves. Simone has seen Logan stand that way, but Reggie is more bull than puma. He shuts the fridge door and greets them.

"You're just in time. I'm hungry." He and Logan do a complicated handshake, and at the end of the fist bump Reggie turns to Simone. "It's good to see you again."

Simone feels awkward. She doesn't do a fancy handshake with anyone. "It's good to see you, too."

"Feel free to take a look around. I'll help Logan unload the groceries and then get you something to drink."

Simone gives the boys a chance to organize and wanders around Reggie's living room while they chat. His place looks clean, but cold. Orchestrated by a competent yet bored mind. Simone bets Reggie hired the interior designer he did because she was pretty and fun to spend the time with. Simone doesn't judge him for it; she just knows this type of interior decorator. Design in Boldene is a very small world. She is charmed, however, by the unique tchotchkes filling the nooks and crannies of his space. They are at odds with the impersonal furniture, and Simone finds his personality tucked away in an old compass, a framed map, random rocks, and broken pots.

She comes back to the kitchen. "I almost forgot, Happy Birthday, Reggie. Thank you for inviting me."

Reggie hugs her. "You are welcome."

Taken a bit aback by the close familiarity, Simone stutters and tries to hug him back.

"It's really the best excuse to convince Logan to cook my favorite meal. You might not thank me later when you can barely move because you've eaten too much."

Simone warms at Reggie's immediate offer to bond with her over food. "For someone who really hates to cook but loves to eat, what you just described sounds like potential paradise. But before I'm certain, run down the menu."

"Buttery lentil daal, fresh naan, raita, basmati rice, three chutneys, potato spinach saag, and chicken tikka masala."

Simone braces herself against the fridge in a mock swoon.

"We might have to work for it. Things could get messy," Reggie cautions.

Simone springs to life and heads to the sink to wash her hands. "I'll do whatever it takes."

Logan empties a few containers into pots and starts to warm them. "It won't take much. I've made most of it already."

Reggie hands Simone a dishtowel and wraps her into his side. In a united front, he and Simone face Logan. "You were right. She's lovely."

Simone wonders what there was to be right about, but she can't help it. She hugs Reggie back, and it feels like she's just made the team.

Logan winks. "Damn straight."

As they dive into the project of making a massive meal, Reggie asks her questions about being an only child and about sewing and the work Logan is doing for her. In comparison to their unique arrangement professionally, what is going on between them personally is very straight forward. It brings Simone happiness to talk about it and soon it is as though she and Reggie have known each other for years.

Within an hour, the lentils are simmering with chopped carrots, onions, potatoes, and broccoli. The basmati rice is bubbling in the rice pot, and all the chutneys are resting in the fridge with the raita. All that is left, is to finish the naan.

Simone lifts her glass from the counter with delicate fingers. Coated in flour, they leave prints on the outside. Logan smiles down at her and hands her another ball to roll out. She leans into him for a moment, not sure how to be in front of Reggie, and accepts it. She takes a sip of the crisp wine and places her glass beside Logan's on the windowsill. Outside, the day has officially faded into night, and now stars dot the cobalt sky with faint flickers. Reggie lights a bunch of candles and fills the room with party warmth.

A quiet knock sounds on the door. Simone sees Reggie walk to it and stop short. He puts a hand to his heart and coughs. Thumping his chest once with a loose fist, he finally opens the screen door and admits Monica. He kisses her on the cheek, very platonic, but Simone can tell he's floored.

Dressed in dark leggings, a black miniskirt, bustier, leather jacket and flat boots, Monica is very composed and dressed up in her own way. Her hair is clean and teased back into a low ponytail. Dark eyes with heavy liner and mascara beneath black fringe, but her complexion is clear and pale. The effect is stunning.

Rinsing her hands at the sink after Logan, Simone dries them and reaches for Monica's outstretched hand. The exchange is warm on both sides; Simone's palm touches an echo of her own energy. There is both conviction and trepidation running though Monica, and for the second time this evening, Simone feels as though she is in like company.

Logan gives Reggie a look of surprise before greeting Monica in a half hug, welcoming her to dinner and thanking her for joining them for Reggie's birthday. "Would you like a glass of wine?" he asks.

"Sure, something white would be nice."

Heat fills the kitchen as Logan opens the oven. The two brothers have an exchange of sorts and Logan's belly laugh turns Simone to butter.

Instead of melting, she pours another glass full of wine for Monica, refreshes her own, and then returns the bottle to the fridge. She joins in as Logan cheers Reggie for a birthday toast. When Logan's eyes meet hers as they touch glasses, there is an intimacy very unlike an employee's regard for his boss. Logan winks and puts a hand on her back. The second glass of wine and good conversation have loosened Simone's mood. She tucks her body into Logan's side.

Reggie watches and grins, giving Simone the impression he was looking for confirmation on something. "My understanding is we have something else to celebrate," he says. "Cheers to Simone and good luck in the coming competition."

"Thank you." Simone blushes and toasts with the others.

Before Simone is asked to answer any uncomfortable questions, Reggie pulls the focus back by saying, "So, bro, how long until dinner is ready? I'm starving."

Logan glances over his shoulder at the oven. The light is on, and they can see bubbles in the naan rising and browning. "I'll add the oil and spices now to the dal, and we should be ready in about five minutes."

The smells of coconut oil, cumin, kalonji, curry leaves, fenugreek, fennel, turmeric, and black pepper fill the kitchen. Reggie paces in anticipation. He stands at the ready to take dishes served up by Logan to the table. Soon, everything is set, and they sit down to a well-laid meal.

Simone takes a bite of the rich blend of textures and flavors and can't believe it only took an hour to make it all come together.

Monica has a similar reaction to the food and turns to Reggie. "Thank you for inviting me to dinner. Please invite me to dinner whenever Logan cooks." She is serious.

With eyes only for the food on his plate, Reggie replies, "Sure, if you agree to spend the day with me like today." Reggie reaches under the table and puts a hand on Monica's knee.

"What did you guys spend the day doing?" Logan asks.

"We drove to the hills and walked in the woods."

Simone can't picture Monica doing that, but likes her all the more because she did.

Monica points across the table at Logan with her empty fork. "You make really authentic Indian food."

"Have you had much?"

"I have. My mother was raised by an Indian nanny, and she lived with us until she passed away. She cooked like this all the time. Where did you learn to do it?"

"Our mom used to cook vegetarian meals for us growing up. She was a bit of a hippie, so beans and rice were staple foods. She also had an affiliation for yoga and read about these dishes in advertisements for ashrams."

Reggie is a little bitter when he says, "She always wanted to spend time in India at a retreat where they served only dal and rice."

"I'm pretty sure she's done that," Logan says.

Reggie shrugs and puts his fork down for the first time on an empty plate. He takes a sip of wine and a deep breath. "Is there enough for me to have seconds?"

"I think I made enough for you to have seconds three days in a row if you like."

Instead of getting up to fill his plate again, Reggie asks another question. "When did Mom stay in an ashram?"

"That first time she went abroad. She was there for about a week, just outside Rishikesh? She sent a postcard."

"My friend Gemma is always talking about doing that," Simone chimes in. "She's way into yoga and meditation."

"She's also really good at baking, right?" Logan asks this question to remind Simone of what she has in her tote bag.

"Yes," Simone stands up and turns to the kitchen. "Before you have seconds, Reggie, you might want to see this." Simone slides a plate of macaroons from her bag and pierces the top cookie with a birthday candle. She lights it before turning around, and when she does, Logan starts singing "Happy Birthday."

Suddenly embarrassed, Reggie lowers his face and smiles. The song ends, and he looks up at Simone, who has walked around the table to hand the plate of cookies to him. He accepts the plate and places it on top of his empty one. The fork beneath clatters to the table, and the room is silent while he thinks of his wish. Closing his eyes for a second, he inhales, and with a gust of air, blows out the single candle. Lifting that cookie off the top, he plucks the candle out and takes a big bite, then takes another one off the pile before offering the plate to Monica.

She hesitates.

"Take one," Reggie says through a mouth full of coconut.

"I have never had a macaroon?" Monica is skeptical.

Simone explains, "It is just coconut, almond meal, maple syrup, and a little bit of chocolate."

Monica shrugs and breaks one cookie apart.

Reggie swallows and says, "It is pretty divine, and I don't use that word without reservation. Tell me you like it."

Monica chews slowly, and a big smile creeps across her face. "Divine." Turning to Logan she asks, "Coffee? Please, may we have coffee with this?"

Logan grins and gets up. Simone stands too and helps by clearing a few empty plates. When she reaches for Reggie's dinner plate, he stops her with his crooked grin. "I'm still having seconds."

She laughs and carries dishes to the counter. Logan is there finishing the coffee. He kisses Simone's neck and asks her to fetch creamer from the fridge. "Don't comment on it. Reggie likes girl creamer, and it is his birthday."

Simone can't help but giggle as she retrieves hazelnut creamer from the fridge. She pours a little into a carafe Logan set beside the sugar bowl, and carries it all to the table. Logan follows with the coffee. The smell is a bitter complement to the savory meal, and combined with the sweet taste of coconut macaroons, the atmosphere is very Eastern.

Reggie gets up from the table to put on some music. He selects Ravi Shankar, and soon sitar music spins the night into a very relaxed place. A plate of seconds and four macaroons later, he declares, "I feel like some Sambuca."

"There is a bottle in the freezer." It is Reggie's turn to look surprised. Logan says, "I have a good memory, little brother."

A bit misty-eyed, Reggie stands up and retrieves the bottle along with four tiny glasses. Immediately he pours all four nearly to the top. "This was my grandmother's favorite after-dinner drink. It's not a shot, just something meant to be sipped slowly." He tips his first glass back and shoots it. After refilling his glass, he looks at Logan, who also tosses his glass back and holds it out for another refill.

"What is with the odd custom and double talk?" Monica doesn't mince words. She looks to Simone for a straight answer.

"I have no idea."

"When we were younger," Logan begins, "and our grand-mother was pretty old, we would all have dinner together on Sundays. She was in a nursing home at the end, so we would bring 'real' food to her and eat in her room. She had a few of her things there, so it was a lot like dining at home. Real plates, glasses, silverware. She insisted on these things in the same way she insisted on courses for dinner and drinks. One night, we had just begun sipping tiny glasses of Sambuca after dessert, when Grandma said after we finished our drinks it was time for us to go. We agreed, and before we knew it, Grandma had tipped her glass back and finished it in one sip. She put her glass down and stared at the rest of us until we did the same. We were gone and Grandma was asleep within five minutes."

Reggie sighs with the memory. "She was exceptional."

Simone nods and out of deference, drinks her glass in one shot and holds it out to Reggie for another. Monica does the same.

Whether it is the warmth of the alcohol, or the effect of a good story, sitting here tonight, with these three very new friends, is exactly where Simone is meant to be in the universe.

She would swear to it. Logan wraps an arm around her and rubs his hand down hers. She scoots in along the bench seat and leans against his side.

"I will get up to do the dishes in a minute." Her cheeks flush with the heat of anise liqueur.

"Nobody does dishes after someone's birthday dinner. It is a family rule."

"That's right." Reggie takes another cookie and looks at Monica. "I'll do them in the morning and reminisce about the beauty of tonight."

"I could help." It is Monica's turn to blush, and the color on her cheeks makes her look like a beauty queen from the fifties.

And just like that, Logan and Simone sense their part in the evening's festivities has just ended. Without a word between them, they both finish their drinks and rise from the table.

"Reggie, it was so nice to spend your birthday dinner together." Simone reaches for Reggie's hand, and he pulls her in for another hug.

"It is definitely my pleasure. Thank you for bringing such a perfect dessert. I'm keeping all of the cookies and will send the plate back with Logan soon."

"Sounds good. Have a nice night. And, Monica, it was so lovely to meet you. I hope to see you soon."

The two girls hug.

"I look forward to it." Monica is openly friendly, and after she hugs Logan, she steps back into Reggie's side. Together they wave good-bye from the small porch.

~

At the bottom of the stoop, Logan waits for Simone. Once she is level with him, about two steps off the ground, he stops her and pulls her in for a kiss. She tastes like licorice and coconut, sweet and bitter like black coffee. A breath into the gentle kiss and

Logan increases the pressure. Binding her body to his so their hearts meet, he presses her closer and his tongue sweeps deeper.

Just a bit off balance, Simone leans into Logan hard and wraps her arms around his neck. "I'm sorry. I don't think I can ride my bike home."

"Let's walk your bike. I'll leave mine here."

"The night is warm and it's spring. A walk sounds wonderful."

Logan unlocks her bike and pushes it down the driveway. At the bottom, he stops Simone and lifts the tote bag from her shoulder, placing it in the basket. Then he laces his fingers through hers and walks the bike on the other side. Able to see a car coming blocks away, they use the middle of the road and walk beneath a canopy of new catalpa leaves. Streetlights glow overhead, and the shadows the leaves make are layered and complex.

Simone shivers and drops Logan's hand only long enough to slip on her cardigan.

Logan helps her and lifts their entwined hands. He spins her beneath his arm and sits her down on the rack behind the seat of her bike.

"Oh no"—Simone stands up—"this isn't a good idea. I've never ridden on the back of a bike sidesaddle."

"Simone, have you ever been to the Netherlands?"

"The Netherlands? No."

"Then you have never seen the streets of Amsterdam, never seen the commuters moving on bikes like fish in the ocean? I once saw a woman with three kids and a buggy of groceries on one bike cruise through a four-way intersection during rush hour without stopping. So, you just sit there and hold on to me. I'm going to ride slowly, at first, so you get the hang of it."

Simone clings to him, and he wraps his hand over hers,

pressing it into his belly. She giggles, and he knows she's loopy. "Don't laugh at me on this girlie bike of yours."

She exhales, and the warmth of it seeps through him.

"Imagine we have just come from the opera. You are wearing that dress, and I'm in a suit. You sit sidesaddle like you are, looking all Audrey Hepburn, and I'll get us home in a fraction of the time it takes us to walk. It has to take just a fraction of the time, because if it doesn't, I'm going to lift your skirt where we are and check to see if you are wearing any underwear."

∽

The next morning before dawn, Simone wakes up next to Logan in a panic attack, again. She is drenched in sweat and her heart is pounding. She is embarrassed about it and tries to get out of bed without waking him. But he rolls over and lifts up onto an elbow. "You okay, babe?"

The endearment draws her attention, and soon she is calmer, focused on the quiet tone of his voice. "Yeah," she sighs. "I'm good. Just caught up in some thoughts."

Logan wraps his free arm around her and nestles her back under the covers. It is very early, about five in the morning. "Thoughts about what?"

"Imposter Syndrome thoughts."

Nuzzling her ear, he whispers on a smile, "Why? Who are you, really?"

"Wonder Woman."

"Yes!" He squeezes her breasts, and he pulls her to him. "Please wear the short shorts and bustier today. Mankind needs your superpowers."

"You'll have to settle for the headband and cuffs. My cape's at the cleaners."

Logan chuckles. "You have nothing to worry about."

Simone rolls over to look at Logan. Cupping his handsome face in her hand, she wonders out loud, "Who would have thought you'd answer my ad and be so incredible, not to mention talented?"

Logan doesn't answer and she likes how he gives her room.

She looks into the depths of his clear blue eyes. "Logan, I'm scared."

Logan frowns and slowly asks, "Of what?"

Simone breaks their eye contact. She struggles with her answer; they are talking about more than business.

"Of course I'm afraid I'll get caught and lose my job or get kicked out of the competition, but I also have a bad track record when it comes to commitments."

"From what I gather, you don't have a problem, it is the people you have committed to in the past who do. You're probably freaked out that will happen again."

Simone knows Logan must have asked Nico questions. "I'm freaked out something bad will happen at the last crucial minute and how I've gone about all of this almost insures it."

Again, Logan just gives her time to finish talking.

"But I can't bail. And you can't bail. I have to do this with you or not at all. I have to believe you will stick."

"Believe, then, when I say this is all for fun and I play to win." Logan holds her hands to him. "Make believe, Simone. You, me, this competition, it is a few weeks out of your life to defy precedent and expectation. And," Logan brushes her short hair off her face, "don't you think it might be fun? That it will be a pretty exciting time?" Logan tips her chin so they are eye to eye again. "Play, Simone. This life is a game. We have nothing to lose because both of us have our eyes open."

Competing is the only chance she has at winning. Simone nods her head.

Above the bed, the window is cracked, and birdsong starts to fill the air. It is otherwise quiet around them, and being awake this early is a gift. Slowly, Logan kisses Simone, and she lets him ease away her worries. She responds well, and works out all of her restlessness by kneading Logan's arms, his ribs, his hips, and then he presses her back into the mattress.

The weight of his body grounds Simone, reminds her this all there is, right now, this moment. Traveling the length of her body, Logan awakens Simone to a bright new day.

16

"*H*ey, Sim."

Simone nearly jumps out of her skin. Aurora caught her off guard in line at the post office, smack in the middle of mentally replaying yesterday. After she woke up with Logan in a panic, she went to work, and then they spent the afternoon and evening at her place. It was their last day putting together the order for Ballistic Bride. Everything came together so beautifully it made Simone want to knock wood. Logan took that literally, and they spent the afternoon in delight. It wasn't until late in the evening that they finished all the details and sealed the boxes closed.

"Hey, how are you?"

They try to hug around packages.

Aurora grunts a little when Simone squeezes her. "What's wrong?"

"I jumped a fence last night and landed on my shoulder."

"Aurora!"

"What? It was an easy gig, super quick! I just had to catch this asshole leaving his mistress's apartment."

"So why were you running?"

"I never said I ran. I just stayed too long and had to jump a fence. I got the shot, though. He wasn't just leaving. They made out on the front stoop first, like idiots." Aurora's green eyes shine, and her red lips bounce, trying not to smile.

Simone smiles for her. She can't help it. It amuses her that Aurora gets such a kick out of catching people being dumb. The whole image of Aurora jumping a fence like a stunt double makes her want to laugh.

"Big delivery day?" Aurora asks, eyebrows arching above her sunglasses.

"Ballistic Bride." Simone gestures with the two bigger dress boxes and the smaller box full of garters. "I can't believe it, but everything came together on time."

"Oh, really?" Simone can hear all the unspoken aspects behind Aurora's comment.

Simone acknowledges the obvious. "Logan is amazing."

"I'm guessing he's amazing in more ways than the one you hired him for. What were you daydreaming about, believer?"

Simone tells her about the birthday dinner, Logan's brother, Monica, the bike ride, the everything.

Aurora nods her head. "So it is for sure more than business between the two of you?"

Aurora is always one for getting right to the point or stating the obvious, and Simone appreciates her candor. "The business part is done."

"I think you are saying the employee part is done," Aurora clarifies.

"I got into Fashion Bolder."

Aurora shoulder bumps her. "Yes! Under which name?"

Simone cringes because the reality of her circumstance dawns on her. "Both, Ficklow *and* B. Clearwater."

Aurora tucks her sunglasses into her tank top. "Well now, that's a fantastic bitch isn't it?"

Simone couldn't agree more. "Both are my designs, but neither one under my name."

"Have you figured out how you are going to handle all the logistics?"

Even though Aurora has the best of intentions, her poking and prodding isn't helping. Simone starts to sweat.

"Look." Aurora puts a hand on her arm. "I'm only asking because I want to help. I'm fairly certain from what you've told me that Logan wants to help, too. This is possible." Simone tries to interrupt her, but Aurora persists. "This is your moment. This is your chance."

"What if I don't win?"

"I'm talking about more than the competition."

And that's at the heart of what scares Simone. A lump starts to build in her throat. The sweating is on in earnest.

"It's too hot in here."

The line is too long.

There is nothing to lean on, nowhere to set her boxes down.

Aurora pulls them out of line and tells the next person to go ahead.

"Sim," she says and takes her things. "How do you feel about all this, now that both submissions are in?"

"I have no idea. Right now, and I don't know the details, but I'm caught up with all the implications. I know they are my designs, but because they aren't under my name I almost feel like it isn't real. Like I'm just going to go through the motions for someone else."

"You are also caught up in a tangle that could implicate your professional integrity."

"This goes beyond being able to pay the bills. Ficklow Fashions is the best boutique label in town. I'm not finding a better job, and I'm not quitting until I can walk out on my own two feet knowing I can support myself." The way she worded that was exclusive and disrespectful to Logan and who he's become to her, but Simone can't bring herself to voice that change out loud yet.

Aurora gives her no slack. "Do you trust Logan?"

"I think so. I want to."

"Are you just scared he'll pull a fiancé and let you down at the last minute?"

Simone nods her head. "I'm scared of taking that kind of chance."

"First of all, that crap at the altar happened years ago. You are no longer that girl. You are now an ambitious professional with an incredibly hot and, it seems, highly capable, lover. At this point, don't you think you kind of have to trust him?"

"If I drop the B. Clearwater entry, all I have left is Ficklow."

"And..." Aurora draws out the word.

"Ficklow's a dick," Simone finishes. "I know."

"No." Aurora slugs her. "Logan's a gem."

~

The rest of the day is spent in total hell. Ficklow demands she find a way to move the entire production schedule for the June Bride line up by two weeks to accommodate his vacation schedule through Europe. The ripple effects of his optimism and plotting around Berlin have her begging favors of every company in her production flow.

In the afternoon, when he tears into her pattern for the Fashion Bolder bridal gown, she calls him out on it. "You could have just told me what was off about it. You didn't have to actually tear it apart."

"Getting precious about paper, Simone? Better precious with pennies than careless with silk."

I can't stand that he's right about anything.

The feeling she has working with James, or rather at odds with him, is nothing like the feeling she has working with

Logan. This is like nails against a chalkboard. He has her questioning all her moves—every calculation, every angle. She is precious over her work because he is careless of it.

These are my designs, she reminds herself.

As the day wears on Simone vows to ensure Ficklow's name isn't on anything that makes its way to Berlin. She wants B. Clearwater to make it impossible, and the only way to do that is to win.

Her intuition tells her Ficklow is making moves. At the thought of it, tiny hairs rise on the back of her neck like they did when she overheard Ficklow's conversation and saw the printout.

If she didn't have designs in under B. Clearwater, she'd question how good a designer she really is. She is sure no matter what Ficklow would have gotten in.

Tension fills her. She breaks the tip off her pencil, and graphite skids across the pattern paper.

Knowing she has to spend the next ninety minutes with him in the Fashion Bolder orientation meeting doesn't make her any happier. Nor does the inclusion of Heidi at the last minute.

Eye candy.

Added to her mood is the surprise of seeing Logan at the meeting. The fact that this blindsides her clues her into the fact that her head isn't completely in the game. Of course he'd be here.

B. Clearwater is his company. You set it up to look that way.

James keeps stopping on the way in to make hellos and introduce her. It confuses her further when he doesn't introduce Heidi. She's left to bridge that gap in his wake, and the resentment radiating off of Heidi is noxious. It reaches another level of offense when it's time to introduce both Ficklow and Heidi to Logan.

She has the most awkward time saying hello without kissing him.

Thankfully, Logan picks up on the dynamics immediately as she introduces him to her boss.

"Logan Clearwater, this is James Ficklow."

James does his best pleased-to-meet-you stance designed to make him appear bigger, but next to Logan's actual size, it's just sad.

"Nice to meet you." Logan reaches out his perfect hand. "Your reputation precedes you."

Simone blushes from her neck up.

Thankfully, Ficklow isn't looking her way. He's preoccupied assessing Logan. "You're the man behind the B. Clearwater designs?"

Simone's heart begins to pound in her ears. The sound is deafening. She clenches her jaw, focusing on Logan's voice, willing him to protect her.

"Yes, I represent a great team," he answers.

"Hmmm." Ficklow is thinking too hard.

Simone holds her breath, unsure what to say or do to break the downward spiral she sees this conversation taking. Paranoia kicks in and she wonders if Ficklow has seen all the competitors' designs.

Then Logan does something she doesn't expect. He turns to Heidi and lays on the charm.

It immediately distracts Ficklow, bringing him back from whatever pieces he was putting together in his mind. With renewed purpose, Ficklow engages in the conversation, finding all the little ways he can to claim Heidi as his, leaving Logan no room for doubt.

Heidi soaks up the attention like a veteran, used to having more than one man fawn over her at a time. She's a good chess player, Simone can tell, because she doesn't let Ficklow get away so easily with the slight shunning he gave her walking through the door. She responds to Logan's wit with giggles and pets, and Simone would have gagged if she weren't so preoccupied with her own distress.

Has James seen my designs?

She can't help but wonder and feel vulnerable at the thought of it.

What if he links the designs I did originally for his entry with B. Clearwater's? That connection in style feels so obvious to me now!

Remembering to breathe out, all she can do is pray Ficklow's memory won't serve him well enough.

Within moments, a small woman with glasses and a hot-pink mohawk hooks up a mic and begins the meeting. For a full forty-five minutes, Simone stands between Logan and Ficklow scribbling notes and jotting down all the details.

Next to her, Ficklow bristles like frost despite the silk sheen of his suit. His energy grows stone cold.

In contrast, the warmth of Logan seeps through Simone's spring dress. When goosebumps start, she folds her black cardigan closed. It is tempting to tuck beneath Logan's arm and wrap her body around his side until this whole thing is over.

~

She's cold. Logan can tell. Almost in response to his thought, she closes the top two buttons on her sweater. The two right over her heart. Logan can hardly keep himself from wrapping an arm around her and pulling her close.

The dynamic between her, her boss, and Heidi is full of tension.

Seeing it firsthand gives him renewed perspective on what Nico and Adam were saying about her workload and time and how much she thinks of her boss.

What a peacock.

Logan shifts his weight. What he wouldn't do to have a few

minutes alone with the small man to simply offer him an adjustment. Knowing it would leave grease on his hands and stain his soul for life, Logan decides the next best alternative is to nail this competition and skyrocket Simone into another orbit completely. Logan is in a unique position, and he is going to help her in any way he can.

Looking over her head and down at Ficklow, he leans in for just long enough to smell her shampoo. She sways toward him until their arms barely brush one another and electricity runs straight to his heart. His pants tighten. He has to shift and break the contact.

Logan memorizes what Candy Bigly says, the woman with the hot-pink mohawk. It is up to each designer to choose whether they want to use students from the local modeling school, or models of their choice. Each designer will make three bridesmaid dresses and one bridal gown. There is a voucher for materials, and expenses are covered up to a point. Beyond that it is the designer's responsibility. Details about how the show will be conducted will be sent two days before the event. It will be held at the Paloma House, a local Heritage House in the hills on the edge of town. They have less than three weeks until the competition. It is not impossible, but the challenge is significant.

Beside him Simone writes fast. From the way her hand-writing has changed, Logan can tell she might be on the verge of meltdown. If it were only one set of designs and dresses she were responsible for, he could see her handling this all like a champion, in stride. But she must complete twice what other designers are being asked to do, plus maintain the workings of her day job.

In that moment, Simone looks up at him. Worry creases the inside corners of her eyebrows. Her mouth is drawn into a tight frown. He wants so much to smooth all of those worries out with his fingertips and lips. Instead, he smiles and bumps into her a little bit. The gesture is playful, and it brings out a tiny smile, but then it fades, and she focuses again on her notes.

Across her body, Ficklow glares at him. It isn't overt. More a subtle attempt to look down on him while having to look up.

Logan raises his eyebrows in mock wonder at what he could have done to offend such an ass.

Above Ficklow's head Heidi winks at him. She isn't his kind of attractive and he's wondering if throwing Ficklow's scent off by flirting with her was a bit much.

When the meeting ends, it doesn't take long for Ficklow to hone in on Candy Bigly.

Logan watches her expression and their conversation with curiosity. Candy isn't comfortable. She ducks her head, shifts her weight, looks out across the room, seeks eye contact with anyone but James. Then her gaze locks on Logan's and bounces to Simone next to him. Candy finally looks back at James. What she says doesn't please him because his jaw clenches hard enough to make a vein bulge in his neck. Logan can see why Simone suspects he might not be on the level.

James spins on his heel and walks directly toward them. Logan looks at Simone. Her eyes widen. He can tell she thinks they've been found out.

The pointed glance James gives Simone makes Logan's inner animal stand up, alert. In his opinion, this charade can only go on for so long.

"Back to the office," James says to Simone.

She tucks the notes beneath her arm and says her goodbyes.

When her lips nearly meet his cheek, he turns his head and steals a short kiss. It's juvenile, and a risk to his dynamic with Simone, but he wants James Ficklow on his toes.

~

"Simone, chill. This is still really new for you both." Willow says.

Aurora and Simone sit at Gemma's table with Willow. They are back at the hearth for Simone's latest Mayday.

"I don't know if I can do this whole partnership thing. He kissed me in front of my boss. We are supposed to barely know each other."

Aurora laughs, hard. Her red lips pull into a beautiful, wide, beaming bolt of amusement.

"What's wrong with you?" Simone barks at Aurora.

Aurora laughs harder. She wipes her eyes. "You expect us to believe that it was Logan who made you look like an ass? He doesn't seem capable of it."

"You barely know him." Simone can't stop the saucy comment from flying out with venom. "I'm sorry. Please, this is serious."

Aurora, filled with renewed mirth, continues, "I wish I could have seen it. He's so big and handsome. I bet you think it looked like he swept you off your feet, all dramatic and everything."

Gemma giggles. She shakes her head, and her blonde curls bounce away from her face. "No way. That doesn't seem like the Logan I've seen at the bar. I bet he did it with such class it made all the girls swoon."

Willow can't help but comment. "I bet it made Ficklow freak out."

"Girls," Simone nearly whines and buries her nose back in her wine glass. "Can we forget I mentioned it, please?"

"I don't think so." Aurora's tone is sober. She takes off her leather jacket and kicks her boots under the couch. "We are overlooking the most amazing part of all of this. Simone GOT IN. TWICE."

Gemma hugs her, and Willow high fives her. Aurora gives

her a look that says "don't you dare move past this moment without marking it in time ceremoniously."

"Right. Got it. Yes. Accomplishment acknowledged. Although..." Simone fills the girls in on the little things she's been overhearing and noticing at the office. "I keep thinking Ficklow would have gotten into the competition even with mediocre designs. There is something else amiss."

"What can it be? You make it sound like we are a coven gathered together to discuss the latest threat to the village." Willow's tone is laced with dry humor.

"Aren't we?" Gemma asks, with mock confusion.

"You are so cute when you act like a dumb blonde, Gem." Simone hugs her. "This isn't so much about a threat to the village as it is about me being a threat to myself. I'm going undercover with my designs and I want to win Fashion Bolder. If I can manage it, I'll have two parallel courses to run right up until the end, and basically have two chances to win."

"But," Willow says, "either way, you aren't winning under your own name or label. I get that the reward looks like it is worth the risk. But just consider your options."

"Enough." Simone has heard enough. "I see two options. One, win under B. Clearwater. Two, win under Ficklow Fashions. Option One is the better for my long-term career because I have a verbal agreement with Logan. He knows he's just the face and the front of the label. I just have to keep him onboard until the contest is over."

You sound like a cold-hearted bitch.

A ringing starts in her ears. Simone gets up and goes to the restroom. She washes her hands and looks at herself in the mirror. All the glow of her time with Logan seems to have left her like a temporary fix. There is tension again in her jaw, her eyes are drawn deep, and dark circles emphasize her hollow cheeks. A knock sounds on the door. If Simone didn't know better, she'd say this were Blues Night a week ago. Only she isn't balling and wanting to throw up.

There is something to be said for that.

Gemma calls through the door. "Simone?"

Simone opens it. "I'm hungry."

"Is that your way of saying you are scared and uncomfortable with all this and you want me to fill your belly with something rich and warm?"

"Exactly."

Gemma loops her arm through Simone's and walks her into the kitchen. Together, they sample the dinner, and her spirits lift with warm food and easy conversation. It isn't long before Gemma comes back around to the subject of Logan.

"So, before we drop the subject completely, I'd like a smidge of clarification. You've slept with him?"

Simone blushes, the sensation of him inside her is immediate. The feel of him kissing her this afternoon is so close. "Yes." She shrugs. "Blues Night."

"More than once?" Willow is suddenly right there and so is Aurora.

"Yes."

"And? You were vague in line at the post office, but there is no excuse now." Aurora is persistent.

"And," Simone says, squirming under Aurora's private eyes, "don't investigate me!"

She lets out a bolt of nervous laughter as Aurora narrows one eye and looks sideways at her.

Returning to her serious face, Aurora doesn't let Simone off without answering her question. "And, what? Is this something that could last?"

"Aurora, please. Last through what? A zombie apocalypse?"

"Practically. Through being both in business and in bed together."

"We are not in business. He's my cover, my front, my contact. That's it. He isn't the brand."

"But isn't it 'B. Clearwater?'" Gemma quietly asks. "His name is the brand?"

Simone is having a very hard time keeping it all separate and together. "The name is just temporary. The rebranding is easy after we win."

Aurora and Willow high five.

"What?" Simone asks, confused.

Willow is the one to answer. "You just said *we*. After *we* win."

Aurora fills in the gap. "You are already thinking of the two of you as a team."

"Okay, I get it. You all are enjoying watching me sit in the mess I've made."

"With Logan," Gemma clarifies.

"With Logan," Simone allows. "If we could just move on from that and talk about the other part?"

Willow chimes in. "You mean the part where we purr down the runway in your designs?"

"Yes. That part. You can keep the dresses as my thank-you gift for doing this. They won't match, of course, it isn't like a typical run of bridesmaid dresses. Each one will be different and custom to your specs."

Willow pours the wine. "Like the dresses you made us for your wedding? I wore that dress until the straps fell off!"

It takes her a minute to realize she put her foot in her mouth. "I'm sorry, Sim."

Simone knew it was bound to come up, and she can see how uncomfortable Willow just made herself. Simone shrugs. "Yes. Very much like the dresses I made you all for my wedding. The wedding that never really happened, but we got to party anyway."

Willow hugs Simone for a long time. "It was one of the best almost-weddings I've ever been to."

Before everyone gathers around the table, Gemma ushers them outside. They collect at the edge of the garden surrounded by the glowing lights in her tree and the tea lights scattered throughout her backyard. Gemma lights a joint and passes it around.

When Aurora hands it to Simone, she says, "I'm sorry, too, for giving you a hard time. It just seems like Logan is a good thing in your life. Helpful, supportive."

"I know, but it was so uncomfortable to have him there, while I had to deal with Ficklow and Heidi."

Gemma takes her turn. "From what you described about the meeting, you might have been uncomfortable not because of Logan, but because you know you are bending the rules and have something to hide. It seems like Logan followed all of your cues and the signs right up until the last moment."

"Yes, and he made a lasting impression. The walk back from the meeting, while just a few blocks down, was curt and cold. Ficklow seemed downright pissed, but didn't say a word to me. He also didn't respond at all when Heidi said her goodbyes for the day. It was almost like his being pissed didn't really have to do with either of us."

Gemma squints her cat eyes at Simone. "Imagine that. Some drama at your job that had nothing to do with you. Don't think I didn't notice you skip over the point. You will bend the rules, sure, but you don't like lying."

Willow speaks up next, interrupting the speculation, and what Simone fears could be a deep dive into her shadow side. "To reiterate the point: You have a lot on your plate, and the least we can do is walk a beautiful dress down the runway and help you achieve your dream. Even though not one of us knows how to do that with any real class."

"What! You can't walk?" Simone assesses the humorless

expressions on the faces of her three friends. "It isn't like that. There are no professional models, but some designers are choosing models from the school."

"And you can't do that because?"

"I don't want the stress of sharing. There aren't that many girls to choose from."

Everyone but Aurora looks all in and ready to help.

Simone knew she would be the last to get onboard. Being the center of attention in any way makes Aurora insanely nervous.

But as she starts to thank them, conditions surface. Gemma and Willow are in as long as they don't have to be the bride.

"Why don't you want to be the bride?" Simone's baffled. "It's the best dress, the fanciest."

Willow rolls her eyes. "It's a jinx, for sure."

Gemma nods. "I'm superstitious about all of that."

Aurora coughs and perks up. "You mean, if I'm the one to wear the dress it is akin to ensuring I'll never get married?"

Willow and Gemma look across the porch at each other with relief. "Sim," Willow says, "say 'I do,' darling. You've found your bride."

Simone hugs Aurora, who barely returns the gesture. "What have I gotten myself into?"

"Nothing you can't handle," Simone reassures her.

"What are you going to do about a third bridesmaid?" Willow asks. "You said you needed three."

"I hope it will be someone Logan knows. Monica, his brother Reggie's girlfriend. Or the person he's dating—hard to tell. It's Nico's cousin." Simone notices the way Willow's eyebrows peak when she says Nico's name. Simone can tell the thought of Nico at the show lights her friend up. For the first time since getting in, Simone believes in Logan's idea of fun.

17

"*S*he hasn't returned any of my calls or messages since the meeting yesterday—personal or professional." Logan paces Reggie's condo. He can't get his brother to concentrate on what he is saying. Reggie is too busy running numbers, setting up trades, and communicating back and forth with Svere to pay attention to what he is saying about Simone.

"Logan," Reggie says, staring at his computer screen, "you are making me nervous. Please, stop moving around."

Logan sits on Reggie's leather couch.

"Thank you. Now, I know you are preoccupied with musings on a beautiful woman, but we are about to close one of the biggest deals we've ever done. Svere will call at any moment, and I need your head in the game." He swivels in his ergonomic chair. "Think biofuels. Think like a venture capitalist."

The phone rings, and it is Svere on the other end. It takes less than fifteen minutes of conversation with Svere and a third party to move a few million dollars and line them up to make a dozen. Reggie hangs up the phone and kicks back in his chair with a huge smile on his face. Logan didn't need to say a word.

"You look quite pleased with yourself," he says, admiring how at ease Reggie is with moving millions of dollars at once.

"I am." Reggie leans back a little further. "Now, tell me what's on your mind, big brother."

Logan dives into recanting his afternoon at the Fashion Bolder meeting with Simone. As he tells him the details, Reggie's blue eyes twinkle. By the time Logan reaches the bit about planting the kiss on her at the last minute, Reggie starts laughing out loud.

"What?" Logan asks.

"Nothing. It's funny!" Reggie falters when Logan swats his feet off the desk.

"Okay, you're right. You need help."

"Not that kind of help!"

Reggie's smile gets even bigger. "It seems to me that Simone is doing exactly what you'd expect her to do if you were listening at all to what Adam and Nico both said."

Logan doesn't need convincing. "But I don't get why she hasn't gotten back to me. Even if this weren't personal, we have work to do."

"Are you sure?"

"What do you mean?"

"Well, you said Simone needed to use your information. You didn't mention anything about her needing you to help her with the work. Maybe you aren't factoring in what she thinks about all this. Could it be she's purposely making space?"

"That's ridiculous." But Logan knows it's true because the reality of it punches him in the gut and deflates him. "Why would she do that?"

"Default response. So it doesn't hurt as much when you eventually disappoint her."

"But I won't!" Logan can't imagine her even thinking he would.

"You sort of already did by kissing her in front of her boss."

Reggie drops his elbows to his knees and squares with Logan. "For all she understands you are there to help her on paper, and the less she gives you in terms of responsibility, the less she has to pick up when you flake or ignore her ask."

Logan gives Reggie a withering look.

He stands up and runs his hands through his hair. The stubble on his chin is just long enough to scrub. The abrasion soothes him. "How did this woman get so under my skin?"

"It must suck to finally face a challenge you can't simply crush."

"I've been here before."

"Remind me." Reggie scoffs when he says this.

Logan winces. "It felt a little like this at the end with Angie."

"Only you're—"

"—in the beginning with Simone."

"What if this is how Simone is? What if she decided she doesn't do relationships?" Reggie is the voice of reason.

"That would mean we are just sleeping together and doing paperwork."

"It would appear that way."

Logan starts pacing again. "That's not enough. I dislike paperwork."

"Logan, this is where I remind you that you can't help someone who won't let you help them, and you can't rescue everyone in need, especially if they don't want to be saved."

"Simone already asked me for help."

"And apprehension at the thought of doing it made her wait until the last minute and have a giant panic attack in your bathroom. Only then did she ask you for help."

"But," Logan stops moving, "she did do it."

"Yes."

Logan starts pacing again.

"You are going to wear a groove in the hardwood."

Logan shoots his brother laser eyes. "How can I make this woman want to fall in love with me?"

"I love that you are asking me for relationship advice." Reggie's tone is sarcastic.

"What about Monica? You seemed to have had a great time the night of your birthday. How did that turn out?"

"You want to talk about cold shoulders? Monica Petrov is ice and MIA since then. Find her at Nico's. Don't divert from the topic at hand. There is no 'making' a woman fall in love with you. You know that. Women have been falling at your feet for years now and you don't even see them."

"It wasn't a goal or interest of mine. Now it is." It is plain as day to Logan.

"How romantic."

"Why the sarcastic tone?"

"You are failing at this with Simone because you have failed to romance her."

At once Logan sits down. Reggie is right. He hasn't taken Simone on a single date. It's been business and then The Salt Lick and his brother's birthday. But nothing proper—just business and sex.

Logan grabs his hat off the coat rack by the door and slips on his jacket. "Thanks, little brother."

"Where are you going?"

"I'm off to see about a car and to get my girl."

"Keep your hands off mine!" Reggie calls as Logan slams his front door.

∼

Logan's 1964 Cadillac Eldorado sits in the bay of Pearl's Garage. Newly painted a pale lemon-yellow, the convertible top is down and the fresh tan leather interior gleams. Nico is polishing the hood, and it is clear to Logan by the way he makes every bit shine that Nico is proud of the car.

"The bodywork is immaculate." Logan shakes his hand.

"It has been a pleasure. I might not ever get another opportunity to work on a car like this. They aren't that common around here."

Logan is distracted from asking Nico more questions about where he learned to work on American cars in the first place, but Monica is in the office, and he can hear her through the door. As soon as she finishes on the phone and the receiver settles with a hard thud, she comes walking out.

Dressed in her usual all black, Monica warms just the tiniest bit when she sees Logan. She gives him a one-arm hug, and Logan can see she looks happier than she did the first time he met her. She might not be as polished as she was on Reggie's birthday, but with a clean face and just a bit of mascara, Monica comes across as almost wholesome.

"Hey," he says, trying to find the right way to ask for her help. "Simone is curious if you'd be up for a bit of an opportunity. I think you might be perfect for it."

Monica looks wary and glances at Nico.

Nico leans against the doorjamb to the office and wipes his hands. "Whatcha got?" he asks Logan.

"Simone's entered a competition, and she needs models for her clothes. She has all but one. It's a simple thing, really. You just need to be able to make a couple of meetings for fittings and be available the whole day of the show."

Monica takes her time answering. On the one hand, Logan can tell she wants to, but the way she chews her bottom lip tells him she also has reservations.

Nico puts a hand on her shoulder. "It's something you are rather good at, kid."

Monica nods. "I'll do it. Simone needs to know a couple of things, but I'll help her if she needs it."

Logan hugs her. "Thank you. I'll tell her. Can I give her your number?"

"Of course." She writes her number down on a torn piece of paper with a Sharpie.

Logan takes the piece of paper and accepts his keys for the last time from Nico. He pulls out of the garage, Monica's number in hand.

⁓

Friday afternoon Logan cruises down Simone's alley. Cranberry trees flood the narrow lane with their sweet scent, and Logan knows it won't last much longer. Their pink petals cover the two gravel paths and concrete strips leading up to Simone's door. Two taps on the door later, and Logan has Simone in his arms. He rubs her back through her sweater, and she tucks her face into the warmth of his shirt. It feels right.

Whatever psychological distance she might have gained or fabricated after the meeting is eradicated by this physical tenderness. Logan can feel it. Her behavior is inconsistent, but he understands she cares for him.

"I'm sorry I kissed you at the meeting."

"I'm sorry I've ghosted you."

"It's okay." Logan tips her chin up so she can see he means what he says. "I know you have a lot on your plate and I want to help you. Is it better to stay and work with you, or do you want to get out of here for an hour or so before you hunker down? I can leave you alone after that if you prefer."

Logan can tell Simone is having a hard time deciding. "It is a beautiful afternoon. Why don't you go slip on something cooler? The day is warm, and I'll take you for a ride."

"On bikes?"

"No, I brought my car."

"Okay, give me a minute. I suppose it wouldn't hurt to get outside for a bit before I go fabric shopping."

A few minutes later, Simone follows him out the door. He can tell she is having second thoughts about coming with him.

"I don't have a whole lot of time to spend away," she says. "I'm ready to get started on Fashion Bolder." Her words are cut short when Logan's car comes into view.

"Wow. Isn't that fun?"

"Let's see, shall we?" Logan opens the passenger door and sees excitement flash through her chocolate eyes.

"It's yours?"

"She's mine," he says, looking at her.

Simone's cheeks turn pink, and she tucks her hair behind her ear before she gets in the car. The top is down and Logan watches her legs as she settles her skirt around her knees. When she raises her face to his, he smiles and shuts the door softly. He gets in and starts the car before draping his arm across the bench seat. His hand reaches her neck comfortably. Slowly, they drive down the alley and onto the main streets of town.

"Where are we going?"

"Just for a cruise."

The drive through town is slow. Tilting her head back to rest in his hand, he likes how Simone watches the trees stretch out above. When they are replaced by unbroken sunlight, Simone closes her eyes and Logan runs his fingers through her hair. She reaches across and rests her hand on his thigh.

They drive for some time in quiet, then Logan turns down a dirt road, and after a few minutes, they park in a clearing full of tall grass. Cutting the engine, Logan turns to Simone. She lifts her head and opens her eyes. He reaches across her and rolls all the windows down. Neither of them gets out of the car.

They are so close to the road, but this area is completely

closed off. Sounds of intermittent cars drift through the trees as the call of birds and crickets gets louder.

"I've always wanted to do this," Simone says, slipping off her shoes and tucking her feet up on the seat. "This looks like new upholstery, but please, don't tell me no."

Standing up, she looks down at his upturned face. Logan smiles at his good fortune. Taking his hand, she steps over the seat into the back and lies down, draping her legs over the edge of the car door and swinging her bare feet.

The sexy sight up her skirt and now the view of her lying across his back seat distract Logan. Turning to drape an elbow over the seat, he looks down at Simone's beautiful face bathing in sunlight. Her skirt has slipped down to pool around her hips. She peeks through one eye and smiles, reaching for his hand. She plays with the ring on his finger. Turning it around and around.

"Where did you get this?" Simone asks.

"I bought it on Craigslist the week you hired me."

"Oh, I would have thought you got it from your grand-mother or something."

"She couldn't drive."

"Not the car, sorry, the ring."

Logan always wears the ring. "It was my grandfather's. So, yes, my grandmother did give it to me. It is very old. It was his wedding ring. I have hers as well." The ring is a gold seal ring. Cast with the Clearwater family crest, it is probably a hundred years old. It is substantial, weighty, and meant to be worn daily. "For a long time, it just sat in a drawer, but when my grand-mother died, I put it on, and haven't taken it off since. I wish I would have done her the honor of wearing it while she was alive. I know it would have made her happy, but it felt too extravagant then."

"It looks very nice on you. It suits you."

"I trust your fashion sense, competitor."

Simone blanches at first. Logan is invested in seeing Simone do really well in this competition. He likes to see her happy. Lifting their entwined hands, Logan invites Simone back to the front seat.

Simone swings her legs inside the car. She stands up on the smooth leather, her dress cascading down. Lifting her leg, she steps high, over the back of the front seat. Then slowly, she puts her weight on it and brings the other leg up to meet it. Spinning on her toes, she steps over Logan and sits in his lap. The skirt of her dress billows around them, between her body and the steering wheel.

The bench seat is spacious and backed up as far as it goes, making room for Logan's long body. Sitting a little lower, he slides his hands up her bare legs, past her thighs, and clears his throat when he finds her warm skin. He sits still with her for a few minutes spent in eye contact. He tries to tell her through the silence all the things he wants to say. Things he is sure would make her run if he said them aloud. She melts a little, pervious to his affection, and kisses his neck, where the collar of his dress shirt lays open. She traces a finger down the buttons. Logan samples the scent behind her ear.

Tugging tiny straps from her shoulders, he rains kisses across her collarbones and over her heart. Logan no longer hears the sound of cars, crickets, or birds. He hears her breath and the pounding of his heart. It speeds up when Simone smiles and unbuttons his shirt, sliding her delicate hands through his hair and around his neck.

"I am so into you," he whispers.

She tips her head back, Logan peppers her body with kisses. When her gentle touch turns adamant, Logan lays her down and presses her into the warm leather with his hands and hips.

High above, the sky is radiant blue. Not a single cloud interrupts the solid color. With her secure beneath the weight of his body, Simone looks him in the eye and whispers, "I'm into you, too."

~

Logan and Simone lay wrapped together on the bench seat of the car. Nestled between Logan's body and the leather, Simone is calm and comfortable. Some time passes in and out of sleep and the music of birdsong and crickets gives way to the purr of traffic beyond the trees. It breaks the spell and Simone comes back to her body.

The affection she feels right now is in stark contrast to how she felt at the end of the Fashion Bolder meeting. Simone is embarrassed by how distant she has been. Logan curls Simone into his side and rubs her arm, kissing her forehead.

Smoothing the panels of his shirt together, she rests her hand over his heart until the connection they have disconcerts her. She shifts and sits up.

"Logan."

"Yes?" He passes her the sundress.

She slips it over her head and turns to face him. His rumpled hair and boyish grin melt her, stopping her thoughts. Some of the things she was crystalline about before Logan are now super muddy. Studying the gentle creases where his dimples draw deep, she realizes there is no clear line between who she was before Logan and who she is now.

~

Twenty minutes later, the two of them stand together in the windows of Vibe, Boldene's local fabric store, comparing shades of georgette in the natural light. Logan convinced Simone fabric shopping for Fashion Bolder together was a good idea. It was on the way home, and he plied her with

Monica's phone number. So grateful Monica agreed and her model issues were resolved, Simone acquiesced.

It was either that or the next round of kisses and licks Logan offered as a bonus and she doesn't think she has time for that.

But now she is wondering if it was such a good idea to do the shopping together. Normally, she is in and out, knows exactly what she wants, and this trip is already taking too long. The translucent material she holds shimmers in the natural light, and Simone can imagine it in the layers she has planned. Logan offers her yet another option, but she has to decline. They have a budget to work within, and a limit as to where they can dial materials up. All in all, it takes them nearly two hours to decide on the fabric for all four dresses. She can feel the time ticking by.

Rolling their shopping cart to the cutting tables, Simone takes a deep breath. "Ready for this?" she asks Logan.

"For what?" Logan pulls a number and gets in line.

"Not what. Whom."

Soon, a quirky old lady wearing a ton of fake crystals calls their number.

"Simone, honey," Roxanne stretches out her name. "Who is *this*?"

"Hi, Roxanne." Logan reaches across the wide counter and reads her name tag as he takes her hand. "I'm Logan, Simone's friend."

"Uh-huh." Roxanne looks over her rhinestone-studded cat-eye glasses and gives him a good once-over. "I bet you are."

Logan coughs back his laughter, and Simone turns scarlet at the innuendo in Roxanne's tone.

Not skipping a beat, Roxanne pushes her glasses up her nose and says, "So what are we cutting for today?"

Simone selects the material for the wedding dress first and places the bolt on the table. It is antique white silk double georgette with a lace pattern in places, very elegant with beautiful drape. It is as expensive as it sounds, and will take up about half of the budget, but it is worth every penny. Simone fell for it the second Logan found it. "Cut us five yards, please, Roxanne."

"You got it, hon." Roxanne flips the bolt a few times and lines it up with the yard stick on the table. "So, Logan, what are you guys gonna make with this? Simone's next wedding dress?"

"Roxanne!"

Logan wraps an arm low around Simone's waist and pulls her into him. "That's a nice thought."

Roxanne looks up, sharp scissors in hand, and nods at Logan. "Damn straight. This girl thinks she's never gonna actually get married."

"Roxanne!" Simone's patience are at an end.

"Well, that's what you tried to tell me last time you were here, isn't it? Bunch of ridiculous hogwash." Roxanne's scissors slice through the silk like water. Folding up their cut of the white material, she places the bolt behind her on the shelves and holds her hand out for the next.

Logan selects the warm pigeon-gray they found for Monica's dress. "Please cut us three yards of this, Roxie."

Simone leans back and looks at his face, surprised he's already given Roxanne a nickname.

Roxanne *loves* it. "Of course, darling. Now," she says, smoothing out the material, "it looks like you might be able to persuade Simone into seeing some sense. Given the way you've got her pressed up against you"—her sharp scissors motion to him like she knows they do illicit things together—"I'm sure you already know just how worth it she is. And by *it*, I mean marriage."

"I couldn't agree more, Roxie."

Simone is startled yet again. It sounded like Logan just told Roxie he's thought about marrying her. *Whoa. Backpedal for a second.* "Roxanne, please."

"This is my chance, sweetheart, to intervene in your personal life for the better. You got burned, that doesn't happen every time!"

"Done right," Logan concurs, "it could be one helluva party."

Confused by how she ended up the odd man out in this conversation, Simone turns to their cart and lifts out the barely blue georgette for Willow's dress. Handing it across to Roxanne she says, "Just three of this, please. And I've already told you, I have nothing against marriage. It's the wedding I'd rather not do."

"Come on, Simone." Logan curls her back into his side. "Ours could be fun."

Stiffening in his arms, she is definitely on high alert now. Simone tries hard not to think too much about what Logan is saying.

"Ha." Roxanne scoffs. "It is a kind of fun like you've never known." Folding the blue material, she motions for the next bolt.

Logan reaches behind Simone to the cart and finds the delicate linden-green georgette they've picked for Gemma. "Like a barn raising." Logan agrees.

"Been there, done that." Simone practically snaps the retort. She doesn't want to be rude, but she is standing right here and these two are talking as though she weren't in the same room. Both of them know her history and still they tease her. "I'll see them soon enough on the catwalk wearing dresses I've made for them, *again*, and that is more than enough fun."

Simone watches thoughts cruise across his face. Handing the material across the table between them, he says, "Three of this last bolt, please, Roxie."

In a desperate attempt to change the subject, Simone asks Roxanne about her girlfriends. While the older woman answers, Simone finds the lace she will use for the straps of the wedding gown. It is full of ferns and spider mums. It is wild and moves with the breeze. It is something Simone has often stopped to look at, and it was the inspiration for her design. Trying not to handle it too much, she waits until Roxanne is ready, then asks for four yards of it. Watching Roxanne stretch it out across the table, Simone has a frustrated flash of jealously.

She is jealous of Aurora, getting to wear this gorgeous dress without needing a wedding. A dress more beautiful than the one she made for herself. She also envies people who have simple relationships, founded in true love, ending at the altar, and sealed with a kiss.

Simone didn't realize what a trigger this trip would be.

Roxanne has practically betrayed her!

And Logan enjoyed it, or at least he enjoyed flirting with Roxie enough to play along at her expense. He opens the door to the car and she gets in but can't make herself scoot to the center of the bench seat. She's frozen and leans awkwardly against the handle like a spooked rabbit. Logan doesn't even try to touch her. He can tell something has dramatically changed.

Simone needs fresh air, clarity.

～

The cold of Simone's silence sits in Logan's lap like a heavy stone. Its chill has seeped through to the core of his being threatening the warmth of their afternoon in the sun. He can't skip this stone and be done with it. It's too significant.

He was very familiar with Roxanne, using her connection with Simone for his benefit. He felt her immediate affinity, felt her to be an ally. He might have known he'd make an enemy of Simone by teasing her.

Teasing her about her wedding dress. About marrying him.

Reggie would be so disappointed. All the romance of the

day has died. Across the front seat from him, Simone sits, staring out of the window, folded to the door. Between them on the bench seat is their bag of materials. At the moment, it feels like the warp and weft of the fabric are the only threads connecting them. It makes his heart ache.

～

Logan pulls up behind her apartment. Before the engine is off, Simone jumps out the door. He follows her. She opens her front door and leaves it open. Caught at the threshold, feeling unwelcome, Logan waits.

Simone busies herself with tidying her space. He can tell by her restless energy that she doesn't know what to say. He wonders if he should go.

How can he make this right?

He stops Simone, grasping her hand by the last few fingers as she passes him by. Her other arm is full of remnants from Ballistic Bride and scraps of pattern paper. When she looks up at him, her expression is so broken, Logan can only draw her to him. He rests his forehead on hers and silently asks her to be still. To reconnect with him. To feel his heart reaching out, searching for hers.

But Simone breaks away. She won't sit still for his peace offering. She almost starts to talk, but stops, and deflates before his eyes.

A truck pulls up in the back. There is a knock at the door. It's a package for Simone. She signs for it without reading it and opens the box as the carrier walks away. Inside is Ballistic Bride's dress.

"I don't understand." Simone checks the package. It's the same box she shipped it in. "Did it ever arrive? It's been opened. This is a mess." She combs through the paper and finds a card inside. It's from Ballistic Bride. Simone reads it to herself.

When she gets to the end of the note, the dam breaks and she starts to cry.

Logan is almost scared to ask. He takes a step toward her. She takes a step back.

"Please, just read this." She hands him the card and turns away. Ballistic Bride is pregnant. She hadn't mentioned it because it shouldn't have been a problem. But it turns out she's having twins and showing more than anticipated. It turns out the dress doesn't fit. Is it possible to make it bigger in just the right places?

Simone is crying in earnest now. She's curled herself up in her green chair by the door. "This order is over."

Logan doesn't know what to do. She's curled up like an armadillo, hard shell on the outside around a soft-bellied center.

There isn't enough room on the chair for him. He stops overthinking it all and picks her up. He turns and sits down in the chair with her in his lap. He knows it was the right thing to do because Simone turns to a puddle in his arms, sinking into his embrace.

Seeking an opening in her tears, Logan waits to say anything, to tell her it's all going to be okay. That he knows how to fix this.

But as soon as she starts to calm down, she climbs out of his lap and onto the floor.

"Simone." Logan won't beg, but he will plead with her.

She won't look at him.

He gets down on the floor in front of her. He holds her face in his hands. "Baby, look at me."

Simone squeezes her eyes shut, tears crushing down her cheeks. "Please leave."

Logan doesn't let her go.

"Please." She says again.

"Simone, let me help you. I know how to fix this."

Simone opens her eyes and looks at him with astonishment. "She needs the dress to be bigger, not smaller. That kind of alteration will wreck the line of the gown. My centerpiece is shot. This was all for nothing. She's going to have to find some dress to buy off the rack and have it altered. I'm done."

"Simone." Logan says her name again, as gently as he can. She's giving up. "Please let me fix this. She'll wear the dress. The pictures will be beautiful. Your work will all come together in just the way it should."

The despair and disbelief on her face say it all. "I know you are good, but this fix needs a miracle. It's just not worth it. I don't have the time."

"You could quit Ficklow." The words are out of Logan's mouth before he thinks them through.

Incredulity burns its way across Simone's face, followed quickly by rage. "I can't quit!" She stands up, brushing off his hands. "I have bills to pay and a reputation to uphold. I have two entries on the line right now. If I quit now, I risk everything. Ficklow will know it was me all along behind B. Clearwater."

Logan watches her work herself into a state. He tries to backtrack. "I'm just saying you would have less on your plate, more time to focus on B. Clearwater."

Simone looks as though she can't believe what he is saying. She sees right through his words and knows he meant more time to focus on me and us.

She faces him square on, takes a shaky breath, and says through another round of brewing tears, "There is no B. Clearwater. It's a name on paper and everything of substance in it is mine. We agreed. Make me believe you are a gentleman and keep your word through the competition. In the meantime, the only thing I need to quit to win is you. I've spent time today I can't buy back."

Her words hit him like a slug to the gut. "I..."

"You should go."

Logan never walks away from a fight. But this isn't a fight. This is his woman, in a state of confusion and despair, saying words she doesn't really mean. He believes this, but he doesn't want to push her to a place she can't return from. She is as proud as he is, values her word as much as he does. It's time to lay it all on the line for the sake of transparency.

"I can imagine how you feel right now, and I'm going to leave. But before I walk away, I would like to say one thing." Simone's face is a mask. There is no trace of the animation he saw just hours ago. No light of the sun filling her smile. "If you peal back all the layers of confusion around us, you will see the truth. I love you, Simone."

A tiny ember burns in her eyes and it takes great strength for him to walk away while she stands there, speechless. Speechless, but not helpless.

She will find her strength.

18

I am not built for this.

After Logan told her he loved her and left, Simone sank against her front door. The only thing that made her move was an overwhelming urge to throw up. After too long spent hugging the toilet, she surrendered to the floor.

The handle on the toilet gleams in the dark. It's the only thing Simone can focus on. She stares at it through the narrow door to her water closet. If she loses sight of that one spot in her line of vision, the nausea comes back. She refuses to throw up more than three times over this.

That thought is total shit. This has to stop.

Weak and shaking, she forces herself to get up, rinse with mouthwash, again, and splash her face. She scrubs at her sundress, wet from the sloppy cleanup. It's grown dark around her. She prefers it; she doesn't want to shed light on the massacre she's made of her reality.

Exhausted and frustrated with the way she is handling things, Simone seeks ease.

She puts on some soft music and takes the tin off her shelves. In a deliberate and methodical way, she makes a cup of tea and sits outside on her porch. She smokes pot and instantly feels better. Less like she wants to cry and be sick over her circumstances.

She calls Aurora.

At first, there is a lot of noise on the other end. Aurora answers on a shout. "Sim, what's up?"

Simone wants to hang up. Her voice is nowhere to be found.

"Sim!" Aurora shouts again.

"What!" Simone can't help it. She shouts back, forgetting she's the one who called.

"Are you okay?"

Simone drops her face into her hand. "I'm..." She starts to lose it again.

"Sim!" There is scrambling on Aurora's end. "Don't hang up. I'm almost where I can hear you."

Abruptly the noise ends. Simone sniffs. "Where are you?"

There is a long stretch of silence on the other end. She whispers, "I'm on assignment."

"You hesitated, Dawn Star." For a moment, Simone is distracted enough to be curious. "Are you sure you're not with your getaway lover?" She visualizes Svere.

"This isn't about me. *You* called. *You* are crying. What is wrong?"

Aurora is so direct it feels like an attack, so Simone starts to shut down again. She wipes her tears roughly, determined not to get so upset again. "Nothing."

"I can hear your throat closing, Simone. Don't smooth this over. What is it?"

Simone tries her best to explain what happened at the fabric store with Logan and Roxanne, then the Ballistic Bride box, finally the break-up. "I nipped it in the bud. It was too complicated. This way it's just me. No one to disappoint, and no one can drop the ball but me."

"Oh, Sim."

Fuck. "Don't pity me, Aurora. Not you, please."

"I can't help it. You shit your nest and know it."

"Aurora!"

"If you wanted someone to coddle you and tell you it's all going to be okay, you would have called Gemma."

"I don't need coddling."

"What you need is an ass kicking. Willow would have agreed with Logan."

"I didn't call Willow."

"Because she would have kicked your ass and said, 'I told you so.'"

"Aurora, what am I going to do?"

"You're going to call Scott. Ask him to read your cards and get clear on what your next right move is. Do you need his number?"

"I don't want to talk to your coach, Aurora."

"Don't try to insult me, Simone. We both know better. Call Scott, ask for cards. Seek guidance from your higher self. I have to go." Aurora hangs up to the sound of breaking glass.

Simone stares at the phone. She tries to call Aurora back. Voicemail greets her.

She is alone with her thoughts, wondering what Aurora is caught up in. She sends a prayer up for her, frustrated that she has no idea where her friend is or how risky the assignment.

Suddenly the predicament Simone finds herself in doesn't seem so extreme. Her career and personal happiness are on the line, but no one is going to die if she is found out, or she bails, or she gets fired. Still, she dreads any of those things happening.

Scott. Tarot. The thought of it scares her. What if the cards tell her what she doesn't want to hear? What if she has built a tower of white lies and it is about to come crashing down? What if the only thing her future holds is self-destruction? What if all of this has been a mistake?

What about Logan?

～

Later that evening, Simone twists the ties on her dress together and apart, together and apart, together and apart.

She's waiting for Scott to call. It's time for her reading.

Her phone rings, and it startles her, makes her angry.

"Scott, you haven't met me, but Aurora gave me your number."

"Yeah, Aurora and Gemma have both mentioned you. It's nice to meet you."

Simone tries to imagine what the girls would have shared with him.

"I've heard a lot of wonderful things about you," he says, reassuring her.

"I've heard a lot about you, too." Simone feels a little bit more comfortable. His voice is soothing and steady. Calm and quiet.

"Have you ever had your cards read before?"

She can hear shuffling in the background. It happens over and over again.

"I haven't." She clears her throat and tries to get comfortable.

"Not a problem. It's simple. I'm shuffling the cards now. When it is time, I'm going to ask you to state your question or your petition. What is it that you would like an answer to or guidance about?"

Simone starts to talk, but Scott interrupts her.

"Don't ask the question now. Just sit with it for a bit and get clear."

He continues to shuffle. Finally, there is silence on his end.

Simone's mind is racing. She wants to ask the right question. The one that will get her the answer she most wants to hear, even though she isn't sure what that is. She feels a pressure to get this part right.

"Simone, you need to relax, okay? We can't force this, and there is no such thing as a bad reading."

He makes it sound so simple, but to Simone relaxing is foreign. She lights a white candle. He tells her to think of something beautiful. She tries and immediately remembers how the sun felt on her body laying with Logan in the front seat of his car.

"We are going to ask for help now, so I'd like you to feel relief. Feel the blessing of support and the comfort of a guiding light. See the God-spark in your heart reach out and connect to its source. See the light finding what you most what to know. "

Just the thought of it brings tears to Simone's eyes. Words like "blessing," "support," and "comfort" choke her up.

"I'm going to ask now that my guides and protectors be with me for this reading, and that your guides and protectors join you. May we all act in harmony to understand what is brought to light. Simone, what is your petition?"

Simone suspends her discomfort and the encroaching disbelief doubt brings.

She finally gives voice to what plagues her most. "I need clarity. I'm overwhelmed. Please show me what to do next. Can I trust anyone other than myself when it comes to making my dreams come true?"

"There is more than one question there."

She can hear Scott deal three cards and turn them all over with a clear snap. A panic starts to rise in her gut. She takes a deep breath, scared nausea will follow and she'll have to excuse herself.

At the right moment, Scott starts to speak. The tenor of his voice stills her, washes away the need to hurl. "You are in a tight position, but it is of your own making. There is a great opportunity now, but also great risk and loss. Opportunity and success are yours for the taking if you are willing to share in every way, with your whole heart. You think you don't want to share, that it isn't in the cards for you—no pun intended—but there is a deeper awareness within you as well that knows you can go much further much faster in the direction of your dreams if you choose someone worthy to share them with.

"You have two options right now, it seems, two avenues to choose from. But one of them is guarded by a villain the other a king. The villain wasn't as obvious at first, he's slick, but the king has been true to form from the start, and that is what makes you not trust him. This person is a bold a champion of yours, willing to do almost anything. That kind of discernment and immediate support makes you suspicious. You've been burned by false promises before and are scared you haven't learned your lesson."

A long pause follows. Simone is speechless; she hasn't anything to say because Scott is so spot-on she is disconcerted.

"Simone, I can hear you breathing, so I know you are there. Take your time. Ask if you have clarifying questions."

"What do I do?" This is her real question. This is what she needs to know in order to move on.

Scott turns over more cards. "Call a spade a spade. Identify the villain, acknowledge the king."

"That's easy."

More cards snap. "There is work to be done. It isn't enough to just know the difference in your mind. You are asked to follow your mind with your actions. Make a move."

This is not at all what Simone wants to hear.

"How?"

Scott chuckles. "Isn't how the ultimate mystery?"

Simone does not appreciate his humor. "Please. The how escapes me. I've made a mess of things."

Two more cards snap. "You have a cord that needs cutting. The villain has you in a stronghold, but I'll stress again, you have tied the knots. There is a bad contract there. As for the king, it is time to offer forgiveness. And it isn't that you have to forgive him. This looks like it's about you forgiving yourself. He already has."

Simone takes a deep breath.

Scott pulls another card.

"Last card, Simone. You are at the crux of your heartbreak. It is time to stop living according to your prior experience, under the illusion that alone life is better than together. Release the past and its hold on your future. Live your life out loud, as your most authentic self. Release the imposter syndrome you wear like an excuse for your behavior. Allow others to delight in you. Allow the King of Cups to delight in you. Until you learn to share in all ways, you will have no true success. It isn't that you won't accomplish things or earn a solid paycheck, but the sensation of victory and the cause to celebrate it will escape you."

Slow tears sink down Simone's cheeks. "Fuck."

"There is more. We've drawn The Tower card, Simone."

I knew it.

"If you do not release the resentment you harbor around partnerships, you will allow your life to crumble or destroy yourself with worry, anxiety, and perpetual fear."

Simone pulls in a sharp breath.

"I know that sometimes, these things can be hard to hear. I tend not to mince words and say what comes to mind, as it comes to mind. It's clear you have dealt with abandonment and fear it now. But you have everything you need. The support is there if you can accept it, and if you do, happiness is guaranteed. It is important to remember that this partnership is different than what came before. To treat this opportunity the same way shorts you of the wisdom you gained from that catalytic experience which led you to this harboring."

Simone has nothing to say. She mumbles something about it all making sense.

"Do you have more clarity now than you did at the start of our call?"

Simone collects her thoughts. "This has been a humbling conversation."

"I would think it the reverse. This conversation could give you immense confidence, and if you take the invitation, you could own your power in all of this. It seems you are preoccupied mistrusting the motives and actions of two men in your life, in particular, and at the same time you mistrust your own strength and spin yourself into less-than-honest circumstances. Trust your heart, first, and speak the truth, whatever the cost. You are a strong character, talented and smart, but you have used your desire for independence as a crutch, and now the thought of preserving it is stunting your growth."

That hurt. The flaming arrow of fact sails right through her. Cauterizing the hole it burned while piercing her heart. It hurts Simone to hear Scott tell her like it is. He didn't say anything new; he merely told her what she knew deep down. The bow and arrow were hers, he just let them loose.

The pain sobers her.

What needs to be done is finally crystal clear.

But do I have the courage to do it?

〜

Logan is back at his window facing out across the valley. He stares at his reflection. Stubble from the last couple of days darkens his cheeks. His eyes are sunken, collecting the purple of sleeplessness beneath them. He pushes a hand through his hair and draws it down his rough face. In the fading light behind him, his apartment is spotless. Every surface gleams, and Logan has even rearranged the furniture. In doing so, he

162

had to consciously resist imagining Simone moving her things in with him. Where her machines would go and how to accommodate the giant cutting table.

Stupid stuff.

Left with nothing else to scrub or rearrange on the outside, Logan is left to address the disarray inside. His thoughts are a jumble, and he can't rest. He keeps reliving the farce of what happened at Vibe and the nightmare of how things fell apart at Simone's. He tries to remember every word she said, every look and sound, but they were hard things to hear, and he isn't convinced she meant them at all.

Logan changes his clothes, swapping jeans for sweats and jogging shoes. He pulls a hoodie up over his head as he descends the stairs and tucks his chin. It is sprinkling outside, and Logan knows from experience that it will get worse before it gets better. That's fine. The weather suits his mood. Damp and dark. He's got to move or his thoughts are going to drive him to do something dramatic.

Instead of heading down the hill and into town, toward Simone's apartment and everyone else he knows, Logan heads for the hills. He starts at an even pace, coaxing his legs into the easy gait of a lope. He climbs the slow, rolling ascent with aggression, pushing until his thighs and lungs burn. Around him the afternoon grows darker, the earth damper. Soon, the rain really comes down and his clothes grow heavy, clinging to him in awkward places. The water in his shoes squeezes out with every step and jump. When he hits the summit, Logan runs off the road and finds the trails that wind out from the clearing where he and Simone made love, under the blue sky. Under the sun.

In the broad light of day, I made love to her and she made love to me.

Within a few seconds of running at full speed, Logan plunges into the canopy of tall trees. The density of tree limbs and foliage mimics the layers of his thoughts and emotions. The forest floor is covered with ferns, the trunks of trees coated in bright moss. The virility of the space fuels Logan. He can't reason with the fact that Simone might not want him, might not even want his help.

He leaps over a fallen log, skidding out through a puddle of mud. The descent down the side of the mountain is a bigger rush than the run up the road. Here, there is unpredictable ground, places where the water has washed its way into the mountainside. Logan runs with the rain, wanting the flow of his emotions to carve the path before him to bliss.

The rain comes down in sheets, and Logan splashes through it. In places, it is deeper than it seems, and each step is an act of faith, the outcome a surprise. The trail isn't as obvious, but Logan doesn't hesitate. The path to him is clear, if unmarked, and soon the road home is visible.

She isn't going to call. It isn't her style. She's done. In her mind, she wants to pretend this is over.

But.

Logan jumps from the path across a creek to the roadside and scurries up it.

But B. Clearwater.

His name and hers are united on paper; the entry is their lifeline. She can quit him everywhere, but there and it's all Logan needs.

He continues to run. The challenging conditions he faces inspire him, and he accepts the adventure. His body feels strong and sure, and his mind calm.

Logan understands Simone's professional ambition; he responds to her desire to succeed. But most of all, he's emboldened by her willingness to risk it all for a wild chance at an extraordinary win.

I want that for her. I want to see the look on her face when all her dreams come true.

19

*S*imone doesn't act on Scott's advice right away. That would be an overt admission Simone has barely accepted herself.

The weekend passes and she cannot make the change. She prolongs her purgatory, immobilized in a cell of embarrassment and fear. She works alone, keeping one eye fixed on the needle and the other on a stack of bills clipped to her fridge. She is much more comfortable facing the challenge of making ends meet than the challenge of asking for help doing any part of it.

Or the challenge of facing the truth and sorting out the lies.

At the core of the truth is what she has with Logan.

The emotional reality of it hits her in all the quiet spaces. When she is spontaneously on the verge of feeling the way only Logan has ever made her feel: free and happy at the same time. Those moments remind her she is stalling.

At work Ficklow and his Heidi are like a dark magician and his muse boiling the office cauldron to near-hostile frequencies. There is a tense current of deceit running through the walls and phone lines, and Simone knows she is implicated somehow.

It knocks on her subconscious in the same monotonous way the pictures on Ficklow's wall knock when he and Heidi eat lunch. It's been happening for a while now. They don't even try to hide it anymore.

They might not be fucking. I can't imagine either of them breaking a sweat over anything.

Simone wonders what Heidi's game is. She is too strategic to be desperate, but could it be Heidi stays for the same reason she has stayed? Because she thinks this is the best little boutique in Boldene and there is nowhere but down, or a lateral move out of a job like this in a town as small as Boldene.

Simone also knows she is using the excuse of her job and too many things to do to find time to call Logan. Knowing full well that his help would change her world considerably. She isn't ready. She can't call him and tell him she is sorry. She has moments of courage. Moments where she wants to call him.

To tell him she loves him, too.

Instead, she spends nights awake working on her dresses for the B. Clearwater entry after work. Sewing alone what they should be making together. It is torturous. Memories from her wedding preparations years ago threaten to crush her spirit. She must consciously resist the impulse to slide down the slippery slope of remembering how hopeful, happy, and in love she was then. She's done all this before and enjoyed it.

Simone tips her head back and looks at the peaked eve of her ceiling. She blinks tears back and waits for her eyes to soak up the sad one more time.

"Sim."

Simone bumps her workbench and spins around at the sound of Aurora's voice. She hops up and throws her arms around her friend, holding her for a long time squeezing her hard.

Aurora grunts.

"I'm so happy to see you." Simone pulls back and looks twice. "What happened?"

With a heavily bandaged hand, Aurora slides her shades down to reveal a black and swollen eye with six stitches above it. All Simone can do is grimace and gently guide Aurora's glasses off. Tiny nicks and cuts are all over her head on one side and her other hand.

Simone steps back, giving Aurora some space and examines the damage. "On the bright side, at least it isn't your lens eye."

"Yeah. It's no stretch to close one eye and focus."

"Can you tell me what you did?"

"Pretend I got kicked by a horse and knocked through a window?"

"Nice. I take it you don't want to talk about it. Sit down."

Aurora winces as she lowers her body into Simone's green chair. She clutches her side and doubles over her legs.

"Are you okay?"

"Yeah, I just got lightheaded. I need food."

Simone digs in her cupboard and finds a stash of toasted cashews. She opens it and hands them over, then offers Aurora some water.

"There is no way you will be fit enough to walk the aisle in a week."

"I can wear shades. It would be very true to form. My form of formal."

"You can hardly stand for three minutes, let alone carry off an elegant stride in the most beautiful dress you'll ever wear. I'm not cruel, I'm selfish. I don't want anything to distract from the dress. Your black eye and stitches are..."

"I'm sorry, Sim." Aurora wipes under her good eye and flinches.

"Third try. What really happened?"

Aurora starts to cry like she's been trying not to for too long. "I wish I could say."

"Isn't this a change? For once I'm not the one leaking tears. You need therapy."

"I need a week of therapy."

"It'd kill you. I'm thinking you need a vacation."

"I'm okay. I am sorry, Sim."

"It's okay."

"I'm not apologizing about the show. Though not having to wear the dress and do all that is actually awesome. Don't get me wrong, I love you. I'd have done it, but yuck. Do you have another model? You have about a week. Did you start the dress yet? I've been thinking what if you wore the dress? It could be the perfect cover for your involvement in B. Clearwater's stuff at the event."

Simone stands up. "Crap." She jams her hands into her hair and pulls it at the roots. "This is such a mess."

Aurora tries to sit up straight. "There is something else."

Simone has no resistance left. With quiet resolve she says, "What?"

"You *have* to call Logan and apologize. How else can you make your own dress? You need his help, right?"

Simone sits down on the rug in front of Aurora. Logan had held her so tenderly here when she melted over everything. "If I didn't know you better, I'd say you threw yourself into traffic just to make this whole scenario possible."

Aurora tries to laugh but it hurts. "Scott pulled the cards?"

"He did. It kind of wrecked my world."

"But then he showed you how to put it all back together?"

"Pretty much."

Aurora leans back in the chair, her lips pale without their usual red.

Simone pulls her head out of the sand and gets Aurora a frozen pack of peas for her face.

Aurora regards her out of one reproachful eye. "Enough procrastinating. You are playing chicken."

Simone wants to get mad, but she needs someone to hold her feet to the fire and witness her doing the impossible. She walks over to the phone and dials Logan's number.

Her mind is filled with racing thoughts, but her gaze rests steadily on Aurora. While she waits for Logan to answer, she asks Aurora a question. "Take pictures for me the day of competition, please?" Aurora nods. Simone musters an ounce of courage.

See? I'm doing it. Watch me. This is happening, right now!

Aurora gives her a thumbs-up.

When Logan answers, he is huffing, breathing really hard. It makes Simone want to breathe hard. She wills herself to stay calm and is rewarded with the deep comfort of her name on his lips. "Simone."

"Logan."

He doesn't say anything more right away. A door slams in the background on his end and the assault of pouring rain ceases. Still, he doesn't say a word.

She clears her throat and swallows hard. "Out for a run?"

"Every day."

Logan doesn't say more. He isn't making this easier on her.

"Meet me for pie?"

"Pie?"

She feels stupid. "Humble pie. And coffee."

"Silver Spoons. 6 a.m."

6 a.m.

She remembers her first phone conversation with him.

He said that on purpose.

"All right. I'll be there."

He chuckles. "I'm not a mean person, Simone. I'll meet you there at eight. Sleep, baby."

Simone hangs up the phone with a very shallow sense of

triumph. And the faintest glimmer of hope. He called her 'baby.' That's a good thing. He can't think the worst of her and call her that.

~

Logan sits down at the soda counter next to Simone at *8 am*. He doesn't like that she chose to sit here, where they are side by side and he can't read her face. He spins on the stool, capturing her seat with one shoe on the foot rail. It's the least he allows himself when he'd rather scoop her up and kiss her or lean over and smell her hair. But she's curled around her coffee cup like an anchor in a storm.

She avoids saying hello by draining another sip from it.

Willow takes it from her and the soft click of the full cup on the Formica echoes in the sparse diner. She still looks at Simone but speaks to Logan. "Morning, handsome. Here for pie?"

Clearly, this is a thing, a secret language between the girls.

"I am." He smiles at Willow who seems to be on his side.

"What kind would you like?"

"What are you having, Simone?" Logan wonders.

"Humble pie."

Relentless, Willow continues. "With cheese?"

"Yes." Simone swallows hard.

Logan likes the warmth he sees in Simone's pale cheeks and can't wait for something other than embarrassment to cause it. She stares into the steam rising from her cup.

"I'll have the same."

Willow fills a mug for Logan. Then she puts two slices of apple pie with melted cheese on the counter, one in front of each of them, and disappears.

Simone takes a huge breath in. Logan can tell she is sick to her stomach at the thought of this apology. She sits up straight. Her fork hovers over the first bite.

Logan puts a hand on her back, between her shoulder blades. The place where her wings are trapped and breaking in their need for freedom. Beneath the wall that binds them, Simone's heart beats. He hopes when they are free, her wings will beat like those of a hummingbird, in figure eights, and she would choose to hover with him for all time.

Simone's fork clatters on her plate.

She turns into Logan, and he wraps her close.

She buries her face into his shirt, and he can hear her breathe him in through a messy sniff. It makes him smile until his dimples ache. He wants to feel her pull him tighter and not let go. It takes time, and time is exactly what Logan has. What he most wants to give and share. With Simone.

"I love you." He repeats the words for her. He says them into her hair above her ear, for only her to hear, one more time. For the rest of time.

He surprises himself by wanting to cry over pie at the diner. Across the shining floor, Willow nods to him and raises her coffee flask in a toast. He smiles again and kisses the top of Simone's head. She hugs him closer before pulling back and blowing her nose into a napkin in the most indelicate of ways.

She finally turns and squares her shoulders to him. "I'm sorry, Logan, for throwing you out of my apartment, out of my space. It was a completely ancient default response to something going wrong in my life. Ironically, ever since then it is super clear how *everything* is on the wrong side of right, and I'm pretty sure you are the only person who can help me make it all okay."

Logan tucks her hair behind the ear she usually pins it above and runs his fingers along her chin, tipping it up. "I'm pretty sure what you are meaning to say is, I'm the right person to help you, and you can see that now."

"Yeah."

"And if you are willing to meet my conditions, I'd offer to help you. Often. Today and tomorrow. Sometimes I'd save you from having to ask, and then I'd follow through. Every time."

Some of the distance in Simone's expression fades. She actually smiles a little, and with a nearly coy turn of her head she asks, "What are your conditions?"

Logan takes her hands in his and holds them so he can put a finger on her pulse at each wrist. Only when he can feel both does he begin to speak.

"Partners in all ways, Simone. In business, in bed, in life. I'm not going to do one, or be a part of one, without the other. When I agree to partner in something, I do it to the fullest extent possible. I'm going to be thorough about every last detail of every last thing we make together."

Logan says these words deliberately. Emphasizing the ones which quicken her pulse the most. When he is rewarded by the dilation of her pupils and the strength with which her life force responds to his offer, Logan leans forward and kisses her. It isn't a slow and seductive kiss. It is a firm press and the sealing of a promise, a prompt for her to reply.

Simone leans forward and kisses him back. She wraps her arms around his neck and stands up to really make her point.

Whoops from the blue-haired regulars go up around them.

Logan smiles into her lips and holds her close. Giving her free rein to let him know just how much she has missed him.

Simone doesn't let go.

She just pulls back a little and says, "Deal."

～

Over the rest of pie and coffee, Simone tells Logan everything. Especially the part about what is going on with Aurora. He was so cool about all of it. When he asks if she's already fixed

Ballistic Bride's dress, she doesn't even get mad. She doesn't have much emotion at all. She just tells him the truth: she hasn't been able to unpack it from the box. He immediately offers to spend the day fixing it, saying he knows just what to do to make it work. The relief she feels is physically palpable, like a lead weight lifting.

As soon as she parts ways with him and steps into Ficklow Fashion, Heidi steps out of Ficklow's office wiping her lip and Simone knows today is her last day. Scott was right—Simone is making her move. She spends the morning getting her affairs in order. They are still three days from the show. None of the day of competition details have been sent yet, so she sets all of her Ficklow Fashion mail and messages to forward directly to James starting tomorrow.

She finalizes the details of production for the June Bride line around his scheduled travel through Europe, and his antic-ipated stop for Fashion Bolder. It all blows her mind, but nothing overwhelms her. There isn't a doubt in her mind Ficklow has rigged the competition. And for the first time, the thought of it doesn't make her sick.

Progress.

This is the final week before the competition, and it is more than apparent Ficklow believes his win is in the bag. Every-thing she has sewn for the competition has turned out beauti-fully. The dresses are classic, typical Ficklow, and *blah, blah, blah.*

Simone is bored by all of it.

When he praises Heidi's craftsmanship and suggests she make travel arrangements so she can be present at the show in Berlin and be sure everything pulls together in the best possible way, Simone takes her out.

Quietly, she packs her bag and gathers her personal items from her desk and the surrounding area. It feels so freaking good when she takes the fake succulent on her drawing table and turns to the pair of them. She offers her resignation, effective this moment. She stands calm, a witness to Ficklow turning aubergine and inside out when Heidi suggests it's for the best. He curses her for the lack of notice when she says there is no way for her to give him two weeks. She has accepted partnership at another label. As she walks out the front door, Simone accepts them for who they are: an opportunistic pair of mediocre talents set on buying and forcing their way to a safe position near the top.

Simone is done playing small to fit in here.

~

For a split second after Simone turns down her alley, she smiles into the sun with her eyes closed. When she opens them, Logan is standing in the middle of the two gravel streaks. She can't help the way her heart skips or the way her skirt climbs when she hurries. She sees Logan catch a glimpse of her legs. She remembers the first time she saw him standing in her doorway, lit up all around like a divine guardian. The deep comfort and raw excitement she felt with him at her table are still there. She rolls to a stop in front of him, and he walks her front tire between his legs.

Logan kisses her, washing her spirit clean from the day, pulling her back into the magical space they occupied over pie less than nine hours ago. Lost in the feel of his supple lips, Simone doesn't remember parking her bike, or unlocking her front door. She only remembers the feel of his skin and how long it takes to get inside.

Logan's grip on her waist is firm. In between kisses he asks, "How was your day?"

The inquisition is homey, and Simone turns, offering the buttons of her dress to Logan as they walk to the shower. "Interesting. Very telling. Dramatic."

Sniffing her neck, Logan tastes her skin. "You smell like spray starch."

"A strong aphrodisiac."

He chuckles behind her ear and slides her gray blouse off her shoulders. He bends her across the middle of the tub and turns the water on for a bath. Hot water cascades into the old tub, and steam billows into the air. She draws the shower curtain almost completely around the clawfeet, cocooning the warmth. Logan unclasps her bra, and she slides out of her panties before stepping into the scalding-hot water. Within seconds, her skin is strawberry red, and she relaxes her head on the lip of the tub.

"You should join me."

Logan wastes no time kicking off his shoes and unbuckling his belt. More water cascades in, and Simone just stares at the growing expanse of Logan's bare skin. Tossing his shirt onto the pile of clothes at his feet, he stands up, tall enough to knock his head on the ring of pipe holding up her shower curtain.

"You better turn off the water now."

Lost in revelry, Simone asks why with the lift of her eyebrows.

Logan doesn't answer, he just steps into the tub and slowly lowers into the bath. As he sits down, the water level rises to within a few inches of the rim, and she scrambles to get the water off. She is dwarfed by him. Logan's legs stretch out, and she sits between them, laughing. Both boldly look at what the water cannot hide. What it has been days since they have enjoyed.

Logan's thighs are heavy and rest against the sides of the bath. Across from him Simone takes a bar of grapefruit soap and begins to wash her legs. Choosing a loofah and some liquid peppermint soap from the tier, she turns and Logan scrubs her back and massages her stiff shoulders. Some time passes in quiet contentment before Logan asks, "What made the day interesting?"

Simone spins back around and looks into Logan's blue eyes. "Aside from meeting you for pie? I quit my day job."

He smiles big and kisses her. Logan lifts her onto his lap. "That *is* a cause for celebration."

"There is more." She hums.

Logan adjusts her hips. "More?"

"You know how the world of high fashion is." She sinks down and tips her head back. "It moves really fast. I've already accepted a partnership, and we are in the running for a big competition."

"Are you now?" He smiles into her skin.

"Yes, we are, partner."

20

$\mathcal{I}$t is two days until the competition, and Simone has asked all the girls to stop over for a fitting. Gemma is the first, and she's early enough that Logan is still out getting them bagels.

"Good morning," Simone says and motions for Gemma to follow her. Behind the screen separating her bed from the bathroom hangs Gemma's dress. It's finished except for the hem. "I wanted to get the length just right, so thanks for coming today."

"I was too excited to wait. Besides, last night was a late one at work, and I was too wired to sleep much."

"Me, neither." Simone is still pink in the cheeks, thinking about the way Logan reduced her focus to just the things that mattered most yesterday. She turns the dress around so Gemma can see the front. "Try it on."

At first, Gemma doesn't move. She just stares at the gown, speechless. Her tawny eyes go wide, and her glossed mouth puckers. "Simone," she shakes her head, "this is gorgeous." She holds it up in front of her and looks into the mirror propped against the screen. "I won't do it justice."

Simone scoffs. "We made it for you. It is to your measurements, so you bet you'll do it justice. And this bustier will do you justice."

Gemma grins as she slips into the dress.

"I see you have conceded some credit to your business partner, the unmistakably hot Logan Clearwater."

"Yeah, he's instrumental."

Noting the double meaning in her tone, Gemma asks, "More than you bargained for?"

"Infinitely."

"Has it been a pleasure?"

"In more ways than one."

"Simone! You had humble pie and made up! Willow told me!"

"I know! I did it. I'm distracted all the time by his sexiness, and yet here we are, cranking out these delicate dresses and marching straight into an incredible business opportunity."

"Sounds serious."

"It feels serious, but unstoppable. I am finally saying yes to the right thing." Simone fastens the last hook and eye on the bustier and then ties the skirt in the back. "It is so unstoppable I quit my day job last Friday."

Gemma's jaw drops at the news. She turns slowly to look in the mirror. The dress is a beautiful and shimmers yellow in the right light. It is tucked and bound in a style reminiscent of Grecian gowns, and the beadwork hits high in all the right places. Gemma swings her necklace over her shoulder and scoops her hair up into a twist. Loose blonde ringlets escape and frame her face.

"Please, Gemma, wear your hair up with bits falling down like that. You look so beautiful." For the first time since she began sewing these dresses, Simone is choked up for the right reasons. The dress has transformed her friend into a bohemian bombshell.

"I will. Thank you, Simone, for this. I'm buying it from you,

you know, and not in trade for cookies. This dress is so much more sophisticated and beautiful than what you made years ago. You are so talented. As soon as the show is over, this dress is mine. I'll pay cash. Hem it, girlfriend."

Simone chuckles and grabs her pins. She believes Gemma. Her work is better. More than her skill has grown in the last five years. Sitting on the floor in front of Gemma, she measures up from the ground and pins the hem in place, just below Gemma's knees.

As they finish up, Willow knocks on the door and drags Aurora in with her.

"It's too early for this," Aurora grumbles. "I'm not even a part of it anymore." She zips up her jacket and sits in the green chair. Her black eye is a deep, deep shade of black and blue, and she holds her bandaged hand in the air.

Willow kicks her shoe. "You are the guest of honor this morning. You are the catalyst in Simone's epic transformation. Without your fuckup, she might have waited an eternity to accept her infinite happiness."

Simone's bright laugh even surprises herself. She hugs Willow hard and says, "Okay, careful now, there are still pins in places. I'll hem it just like Gemma's to hit where you want it, but I have ideas."

Willow closes her eyes as Simone lifts the straps of her dress and she slides her arms through. Gently zipping up the back, Simone looks in the mirror to catch what Willow's reaction is.

Willow opens her eyes slowly. The sky-blue fabric is a perfect complement to Willow's red hair, and the color makes her eyes pop. The spaghetti straps are peppered with crystals and the cascading folds of fabric fall away from her fair skin in graceful sweeps.

"Is it short enough?" Simone turns Willow around so she can look into the floor-length mirror she has propped against the wall. "I'd like to hem it mid-thigh. You have great legs, let's show them off?" Simone is hoping Willow thinks of Nico before she answers.

On a deep sigh she says to Simone, "It is absolutely stunning." Rotating so she can look over each shoulder at her low back and the glowing material, she shimmies a little to see it move. The girls catcall. Light glimmers across the weave, and the georgette sways a little once Willow stops dancing. "I wish all bridesmaid dresses were so flattering."

Basking in the compliment, Simone responds, "Thanks. Hearing that means a lot."

"You know, I have always liked the things you make, but this is in another class altogether. Put the hem where you think it will make the dress look best." Willow flashes a leg just as Logan steps through the door, his hands full of food.

He whistles and says, "Nailed it, Simone."

She smiles and motions for Willow to turn around so she can unzip the dress.

"Wait a second." Logan dries his hands off and walks over. "Let me get a look."

Willow smiles brilliantly and does a slow turn.

Simone and Logan only have eyes for the dress. Watching it swing and settle, they both make mental notes about how to finish it cleanly.

"Okay," Logan says and heads back to the little counter. "I won't look."

Willow steps out of the dress and gets her work uniform on while Simone hangs it up. "I still can't believe this was a sheet of material just a day ago."

"Have you finished the bridal gown yet?" asks Aurora.

"No, but Logan says it is nearly there."

"Just the finishing touches left," Logan says and hands around a plate of bagels and spread.

Willow grabs a bagel and her bag.

Aurora stands up.

"Anyone staying for food?" Logan asks.

Aurora shakes her head. "I've got to catch a plane. Willow made me come here in exchange for a ride to the airport."

"You'll be back in time for the show?" Simone asks, silently reminding Aurora she agreed to take a few photos for her.

"Of course."

Willow loops her arm through Aurora's good one and says, "We are off, but I'll see you, Sim. tomorrow night, right?"

"Yeah, spa night." She turns to Gemma. "Still up for bringing the snacks and your nail and henna stuff?"

"I already made the food and set everything aside. I'll be ready for a spa night."

Simone and Logan wave the girls off, and before they know it, Monica and Reggie pull up in back.

~

Late morning light pours into Simone's garage, and the front door is open. Music fills the room, and Logan stands at the counter making morning Bloody Marys for Simone, Reggie and Monica. Spooning horseradish and black pepper into the last glass, he stirs it with celery and hands it over to Monica.

Reggie accepts the second glass Logan offers and says, "What are we celebrating?"

"A wedding."

Reggie chokes on his first sip, and Logan pats him on the back while he coughs.

"Don't scare him." Simone joins them at the kitchen counter, kisses Reggie's cheek, and slips under Logan's arm. "We shipped Ballistic Bride's dress this morning, and everything with her order was perfect. Thanks to Logan."

Holding up his glass, Logan grins at Reggie and says, "Cheers. To garters and girls."

Reggie touches his glass. "To girls and gams."

Simone raises hers. "To gams and glitter."

Monica reluctantly adds, "To glitter and guns?"

"Gunmetal gray, to be exact," Simone says and takes a sip. Turning to Monica she says, "That's the color of your dress. Thank you for coming this morning. We appreciate your help."

"Of course," Monica stretches the vowels out in her way, "but let's try on the dress before you thank me."

"Well said." Logan winks at Monica. "Show it to her, Simone."

Simone takes Monica's arm and draws her over to the screen separating her bath and bed. Hanging on the back is a simple, long-sleeve wrap dress in a silvery-gray georgette. Monica looks at the dress and goes quiet.

"I know what you're thinking," Simone whispers, "but just try it on and I'll show you my ideas."

While Monica changes behind the screen, shedding long, dark layers of clothing, Simone opens a sketchbook to pages with patterned flowers. Stylized blooms inspired by henna tattoos are scattered across two pages. "I have a friend who is really good with henna. She's in the show, another bridesmaid, actually, and she's agreed to do this for me. I'm planning on having everyone over tomorrow night to sort of start the party, and we could take the time then to integrate these with your tattoos. I might ask everyone to wear one."

Monica looks over the designs. "Well," she says, looking surprised, "yeah, I think that might work."

Not wasting any time while Monica decides, Simone opens up the wrap dress and slips Monica's arms into it. The long sleeves bell very low and close at the wrist, completely covering long scars on her forearms. Snapping the first flap closed on the inside and then tying the simple belt at the other side of Monica's waist, Simone then turns her new friend to look in the mirror.

Against Monica's gray eyes and heavy black bangs, the pigeon-gray double-silk smolders. The dress is on the verge of being too short, but that is only because Monica has very long legs. Running up the length of both of them are barbed wire tattoos. Monica isn't incredibly tall, but her proportions are short in the waist, so this cut looks very flattering on her.

Simone can tell she is surprised by the fit and the way it seems to soften her features and expression. Monica draws in a breath and silently lets it out. She walks to the mirror in a slow, practiced step, turns, and looks over her shoulder.

From across the room, Simone watches Reggie study Monica's moves as she makes the dress look like water.

"I'm thinking of using sepia, as black henna will be too harsh with the rest of the dresses, and sepia will look good with your ink. What do you think?"

"Yes. It will be fine. This dress is very lovely." Monica skims her hand down one sleeve, and the silk swims against her skin. Her expression darkens for a moment. "Thank you."

"Monica, I'm the one who is doing the thanking here, okay?" Brushing the material smooth across Monica's shoulders, Simone tests the length of the sleeves and finish on the hem. The only beads on this dress are at the tassels of the belt. It is simple and understated in a way that flatters Monica's frame and considers her edgier look.

Logan joins the two women and spends a few minutes noting changes in the side seams. "I say you wear your jewelry and do your own makeup."

Wrapping Logan's arm over her shoulder, Simone continues, "Yeah, weddings are too often about the bride making every one of her maids look like they fit a magazine shoot. That's not what we're going for. We want a cohesive look, but unique features. You've got your own thing going, and so do Gemma and Willow. You'll meet everyone Friday. Well, almost everyone."

Monica looks over her shoulder in question and Simone answers, "Aurora has a black eye that is swollen shut and she broke her hand, so I'll wear the other dress. Aurora's taking the pictures."

"Wait," Reggie says, joining them before the little mirror, "I thought she was the bride?"

"She was." For the first time, Simone questions whether she is superstitious.

~

It's the night before the competition and the big door to Simone's garage is open. The little lights around her porch are cheery and bright. Inside, tea lights flicker on every surface. Set in tiny dishes and old jars, they fill the space with a warm glow. On the paper screen occluding the bathtub hang four dresses. The beads on each of them shimmer and shine in the moving light.

Simone's worktable is clear for the first time in weeks, and an old embroidered tablecloth with huge flowers is spread across it. Suddenly, her apartment is full of her friends, and Simone is more than ready to celebrate.

Gemma's arms are loaded, and it takes her a minute to set things down in Simone's sink. "It amazes me that Logan finds a way to cook in this lack of a kitchen." Gold hoops swaying big, Gemma shakes her hair back and fishes a large platter out of one of her canvas bags. She places it on the only square foot of counter space and begins to set up her chocolate fondue fountain and assorted dippers.

"What happened." Simone isn't asking a question; she's making a statement. Fondue only happens at times of emergency and high stress for Gemma.

"I don't want to talk about it."

"Gem," Willow gently prods.

"I can't talk about it." Gemma lights a fire under the pot and begins to coax huge chunks of dark chocolate into melting. Absentmindedly, she picks up a ladyfinger and dips it into the sauce.

Simone snags a ladyfinger and chases Gemma's dunk. "If you don't shed your bad attitude like a set of running stockings right now, I'm calling Adam."

Stopping mid bite, Gemma turns to Simone. "How did you know?"

"I didn't know, but now I do."

Gemma turns the fire down low and carries the platter to the workbench. "I thought for sure you'd spoken to Aurora."

"*You've* spoken to Aurora?" Simone is incredulous. "She's been MIA since you all left the other morning."

"I never call her, so she picked up right away. It's like she knew I was on a freak out. Anyway, let's not talk about me. Let's talk about you."

Willow pops the cork on a bottle of Prosecco and pours the glasses. Handing one to each girl, she holds her own high and begins a toast.

Monica knocks on the door just as Willow's about to say something.

"Perfect timing." Willow quickly pours the last glass. "I'm Willow," she says as she hands it to Monica, "and this is Gemma."

"Nice to meet you." Gemma raises her glass and takes a huge gulp.

Simone gives Monica a hug and nods to Willow, who continues, "Tonight is something special. Tomorrow is sure to follow. So bottoms up, ladies, let's open another bottle."

All the girls raise their glasses, and as Gemma finishes hers, Simone warns, "No hangovers."

Gemma shrugs and pours herself another glass. "I'm thinking I should just keep this buzz up and then quit after one more glass. I need to be off balance for just another breath or two."

"It got hot and heavy with Adam?" Simone can't think of any other way to get to the heart of the matter.

Willow says, in an aside to Monica, "Adam is Gemma's boss at The Salt Lick."

"Ahh, Nico's friend with the mustache." Monica sips her bubbles. Willow does a second take, like she only now remembered Monica is Nico's cousin. Simone is really enjoying this. Tomorrow is going to be good.

Gemma distracts them by unloading the other canvas tote she carried in with her. "Who's first? I've got enough colors here to suit everyone, and I think, Simone, that you want to go for nudes, right?" Gemma opens a case of cosmetics and nail polish that would impress any makeup artist. She looks up and consequently directly at Monica, who assesses her spread like she knows what she's looking at. "What," Gemma asks, "it's a hobby."

"Gemma!" Simone scolds her. "You snapped at someone you've just met! Something big has happened. You must've slept with him!"

"We didn't sleep."

Willow reaches for her phone and plugs it into Simone's speakers. The Band kicks in with "Ophelia" and the lyrics aren't lost on Gemma.

She glares through thick, dark lashes at Willow. "I did the math, read the charts. It was a one-time gig. It won't last, and I've most likely lost my job. I left in the morning before he could tell me to get out."

"You didn't." Simone turns the music down a bit, and even Willow's joy is slightly dampened.

Gemma dunks a ladyfinger deep into the chocolate, waiting until it nearly falls apart before she shoves the whole thing in her mouth at once.

"Oh, I did," she sputters through a mouthful.

"All right, sister, I'm cutting you off." Willow tries to pull her away from the fondue by topping off her champagne. "Give us the details."

"What details?" Gemma asks around another cookie and chocolate. "I had a great shift, and during closing I drank too much tequila." She wanders off in thought. "Somehow I leapt across the bar to jump his bones. Then I bolted, but at the bus stop Aurora answered her phone and I got distracted. Adam stepped out front to close the door to the bar. As soon as he saw me, and I saw him, it was like I had no governor." Gemma leans against the counter in the kitchen and covers her face in her hands. Through a shield of pale polish, she confesses, "I called in sick to work for the first time ever last night, I am so embarrassed."

The Band has long since finished playing, and now there is a thick silence.

Monica sets down her glass and reaches for Gemma's hand. The hint of jagged scars on her forearm peek out from beneath her leather cuff. She turns Gemma's hand over. "This color's nice. Just like champagne. Would you mind painting mine? I don't have a steady hand anymore...done too many embarrassing things in life I have yet to forgive myself for."

Gemma sees the scars.

Tears well up in her eyes, but she bats them away. On a sniff she says, "Fuck it. I'm getting drunk. This color is 'Chiaroscuro' and it would look great on you."

Simone shrugs. The only person she knows who can rock a hangover like a model is Gemma.

"Girl," Willow says as she rubs Gemma's back, "no sense in lamenting what can't be changed. Ride this wave, take his cue. Good jobs come and go, but good friends never do. If Adam is worth your time, and I believe him to be, he'll come back around."

~

Logan arrives late that night, after he is sure the girls have gone home and Simone has soaked for an hour in the tub. He greets her with an enormous bunch of flowers from the field where they made love in the Cadillac. Accepting the blooms, she folds them in her arms and breathes them in. Her crush releases their scent, and it is as pungent as it is sweet.

Simone looks up into his eyes, and Logan can see how much she enjoys his gift. Cupping her face in his hand, he tilts her head back and kisses her. Softly at first, and she returns the pressure. He can tell she's had a lovely time with her friends. Her energy is luminous and bouyant. She is fresh and scrubbed smooth, all pink in the perfect places.

Threading her hand into his thick dark hair, she pulls him close and really kisses him.

Logan hadn't anticipated how much the flowers would turn Simone on, but he is ready when she rises on her toes and melds her body to his. Crushing the flowers between them, Logan doesn't resist the pull of her body. Spicy blooms fill the air around them. He lifts Simone off the ground, nipping at her neck and collarbone. She buries her face in his shoulder and wets his shirt with her tongue.

They cross the room, and Logan skirts the edge of the work-bench, laying Simone down on her bed. She opens her arms and reaches for his t-shirt, drawing it up and over his head. Flowers fall everywhere between them. Logan slips the tie on her robe free, and when it is open, she is bare to him. He palms her breast, covering it completely. It is a possessive gesture he follows with licks of his tongue and a tight pinch. He touches her everywhere, and she returns the favor, skimming her hands down his body. For a long time they love each other slowly, patiently.

Everything has been done. All the work is finished. This is the time for play. This is the real show. This is what I have been talking about all along.

"I understand now," she says and kisses him until she falls asleep all wrapped up in him.

When she wakes up early the morning of the competition, a small bunch of wildflowers tied together with a white ribbon sit on the pillow beside her. Looped into the knot is a platinum Art Deco engagement ring.

"It was my grandmother's." Logan sits at the foot of the bed, watching her carefully.

"The mate to the ring you wear now."

"Yes."

"It's beautiful."

"You'll marry me, then?"

Simone props herself up on her elbow and reaches for the flowers. She smells them and unties the knot. The ring sparkles at her fingertips.

Logan takes the ring from her and kneels at the bedside. "My daredevil sprite, I have loved you from the moment I first saw the freckle by your belly button. Take a chance and say you'll spend the rest of your life with me?"

Any minor glitches in his conviction fade with the smile and glow of pink flooding Simone's cheeks. This is the best way to make her blush.

"Yes," she whispers.

21

*L*ogan and Simone walk up the porch steps to Paloma House, an old home not far from Logan's Victorian. A modest porch wraps around the first floor of the three-story house and spills out down a set of stairs to a balcony in the back overlooking the hills below. The centerpiece of the house is a generous front door with a stained-glass pattern in light blues, yellows, and grays. Shaped into a bird and his cascading tail, the glass oval nearly fills the dark, heavy door. Before they get a chance to knock, it opens inward and a short bottle blonde motions them in while she listens to someone on the phone.

"Label?" she asks without any easy chat.

"B. Clearwater," Simone answers and the blonde ushers them into the back.

Stuck for a minute waiting for two other people with a ladder to pass through the hallway, Logan and Simone look up. Above them is another beautiful stained-glass image of two birds, in the same colors, entwined. Light pours through the couple and shines on the black and white tile floor beneath them. Before they get too much of a look at the stage and props set up for rehearsal, Logan and Simone are nearly pushed out of the way toward the kitchen in the back. On a big island in the center are coffee and pastries. Simone pours them each a mug, and they lean against a counter, waiting for the other contestants to arrive.

This meeting is a lot more serious than the last. He can see apprehension and tension on the faces of more than one hipster in the room. Logan stretches an arm out behind Simone on the counter and sips his coffee. Relaxing, he crosses his legs at the ankles and takes a minute to look around.

At the last minute, Ficklow and Heidi walk in, the picture of tight and cold professionalism. Logan pulls Simone in closer, and when Ficklow finds him in the crowd his face turns a furious shade of fuchsia. He has no comeback. Simone is here on behalf of one company only. Logan has to resist the impulse to laugh.

Simone actually does. The sound of it fills Logan with joy.

This capable woman beside him could have been a ball of worry and tension and sheer nerves this morning. Strung out between two high wires and falling off both. But instead, here she is. By his side. His partner. In all things. He made sure of that this morning. Whatever else happens today is icing on the cake. Logan knows that Svere, Reggie, and Adam are all planning on being here today. Whether B. Clearwater wins or not won't be the only thing determining the success of the brand. There are capitalists waiting in the wings, on the lookout for their next investment.

If Logan has any say, and he does, this next year of Simone's life, and his life, will be incomparable.

$\sim$

Later that morning, Simone sits cross-legged steaming the hem of Willow's dress who stands next to her in a robe and flip-flops drinking tea. Gemma's adding a couple of sticky rhinestones to the henna she painted on Monica's tattoo last night. A series of wild roses cruise up her legs along the barbed wire, and it has the effect of adorned stockings.

"Those turned out really well." Simone glances at Monica's leg and then up at her face. Monica is perfectly made-up, with heavy liner on her upper lids, lots of mascara, and a nearly nude palette everywhere else.

Willow sees the sparkle and grabs Simone's hand. "What's this?"

Simone smiles. "This is probably as good a time as any to tell you all I'm engaged. Logan must be crazy."

A flurry of activity surrounds Simone as the girls get a look at her ring and ask all the questions. Willow threatens to start crying until Gemma begs her not to wreck her makeup, and Aurora captures all the mayhem in stills.

Finally the girls help Simone into her dress. The big standing mirror in the bay window makes for a perfect setting, and Aurora's practiced eye captures just the right details and angles for B. Clearwater's catalogue to come.

Logan's been downstairs, checking on the timing and final details. When he finally makes it back upstairs to cue the girls, he enters their room to a round of applause and finds Simone nesting the headpiece at her hairline. Gemma's just finished her hair and makeup. There is barely anything there, just a hint of sheen and sparkle. Simone is glowing.

"Simone."

Simone turns and looks at Logan, feeling hopeful. It's the first time they have seen the entire look all pulled together: dress, headpiece, shoes, finishing touches. And Simone is simply shimmering all over. The dress fits her like a glove and pools around her feet. Logan's last-minute alterations have made the dress truly hers.

Simone searches his face, trying to read his expression.

Logan's eyes cruise down her body and back up, but she is aware that he isn't looking at the dress. He's looking at who's wearing the dress.

"You are beautiful. Really, truly beautiful."

Gemma and Willow step back and join Monica. Every now and then, Aurora snaps a picture or two, but the room is silent and the house buzzes all around them.

Simone laughs, and the levity brings with it tiny tears of relief. She takes a deep breath. She has imagined this moment with Logan differently, but this is so incredibly right. She looks at her friends, all so beautiful in their own way, wrapped up in her clothes. The stage is set, the important players are on and ready. All they have to do is play nice with Ficklow.

And Ficklow sinks his own ship. It isn't even hard for Simone to watch those designs walk down the runway before the B. Clearwater designs do. They aren't really hers, after all. She is at peace with the fact that she doesn't have to claim any ownership over something she had to compromise on, water down, and strip of all her personal charm. In the place of any jealousy she might have once felt at the way Ficklow paraded Heidi around, Simone now feels pity. Heidi isn't happy, and as the day wears on, it is obvious the honeymoon for her and Ficklow is over. He has a temper tantrum when Ficklow Fashion doesn't win, and the embarrassment Heidi shows at his childish display speaks volumes.

When Simone walks behind her friends through the crowd on the wraparound porch, she truly feels like a bride. And this time, her groom is waiting for her when she reaches the end of the aisle.

EPILOGUE

*A*urora leans back, resting her head against the flight of stairs behind her. It is throbbing, and the pressure behind her black eye is building. Out of the corner of her good eye, she sees Logan dip down and steal a kiss from Simone as they enter the foyer from the kitchen of the Paloma House. The newest winners of Fashion Bolder's spring competition, B. Clearwater made quite a mark on the judges. Now, as late light pours in through the stained glass above, they are lit up and Simone is obviously happy.

Aurora lifts her lens, and without looking snaps the picture, certain the beautiful subject matter will compensate for any technical imperfection.

A glass of champagne floats down from above, and when Aurora looks up, she sees the face of her dear friend Gemma.

"Hey, trooper, help me make good on this bottle of bubbly I commandeered all for myself."

"Can't. I'm on the job."

"Bullshit. Toast. Your face looks terrible," Gemma says without mincing words.

"Thanks, friend, you're looking beautiful, too." On

impulse, Aurora tries to wink, but it causes such an earthquake of pain across her features. Staring at the parquet floor before her, Aurora focuses on the pattern and then Gemma's suede pumps appear. Aurora takes another photograph, and then snaps a series of the feet of all their friends milling about the main floor of the house. A blues band plays in the living room, and people are starting to dance. The day is fading now and merging with the glow of street lamps outside.

The crowd from the competition has thinned to mostly participants and their friends. Around them burn a bunch of white candles. The winner's excitement of earlier has mellowed now into a lover's burn.

The romance of it all makes Aurora uncomfortable.

Everyone is here but Adam Bear and Aurora wonders what Gemma thinks about that. From what Aurora can tell, Willow and Nico might actually make out tonight. Even Svere, who took her hint, is here but has left her alone, avoided her all day —much to both her relief and her disappointment. It is too hard to feign emotional distance when she is near him. It is easier to physically avoid him like she has in the past.

The breech of their deal at The Salt Lick on Blues Night, when he made a pass at her in front of everyone, isn't something she had anticipated. They are undercover lovers. Period. A safe getaway lay without consequence. She needs tight boundaries around her personal life. She has her mom and her career. Svere doesn't fit in on the *inside* of her life. He's upper class, dialed in, generationally wealthy and Aurora is light years behind him. It is undeniable: what has been going on between them must end.

Gemma tops off her glass. The music gets a little louder. In a corner of the foyer, Logan crouches and frees the caught up hem on Simone's skirt. Aurora takes another series of casual photos as he lets go and skims her backside, taking her hand.

He leads Simone to the middle of the large floor, and they begin to dance.

Gemma looks at Aurora with happiness and a twinge of something closer to envy before toasting her and promptly finishing her glass. In a short amount of time, the bottle is empty, and it is Aurora who goes in search of another.

Wandering back toward the kitchen, she stumbles upon Monica and Reggie making out in the pantry. Out of habit, she snaps a covert photo, shuts the door for them, and keeps walking. A group of people she doesn't know are huddled around an island in the big kitchen. Candles float in clear bowls of water on every surface and shadows dance. Aurora opens the fridge and helps herself to a bottle of Prosecco. She grabs a cloth napkin and steps out the back door.

The backyard is musky and damp, a little chilly. New greenery is everywhere. She stands the bottle up on the balcony railing while she shakes a cigarette free and lights it. Before she's had a complete drag and opened the bottle, the screen door bangs open behind her.

But it isn't Gemma come to join her.

It is Svere who steps out onto the porch. "Hey, stranger."

Aurora can't move.

Rising smoke makes her good eye burn.

Pressure builds behind the cork in her hand.

On a muffled burst, it pops.

~

The end.

To find out what happens next for Aurora and get notified about the release date of COPPER: a Boldene Romance (Book 2) SIGN UP FOR MY NEWSLETTER at www.estherstar.com!

You will also get FOOLS FOR LOVE, a Boldene Romance PREQUEL for the series.

Continue on to read more about COPPER: a Boldene Romance (Book 2).

ESTHER STAR'S INNER CIRCLE

Every girl deserves a circle of friends they can love and trust. I want this for myself, and I want this for you, too. Over the years I've gathered close to my heart women who make me a better person, and ask me to show up as my true self, time and time again. It isn't easy, but their friendship is my parachute on this wild ride, and I'd like my friendship to be your parachute, too. If you have read this far, I bet you are with me on this.

FOOLS FOR LOVE, a Boldene Romance Prequel gives you a sneak peak into the friendship of Simone, Aurora, Gemma and Willow. Please sign up for my mailing list at www. estherstar.com and I'll send you a free copy of it!

All in all, I'm a pretty private person and don't share much on social media except for pictures of my darling kitten, MasQuerade (IG: @esther_star_author). But in the Inner Circle, I'm more of an open book. It takes a little more effort to become a part of but it's easy. Go to: www.estherstar.com/inner-circle/. There I do monthly tarot readings and coffee chats and whatever else we decide we need or want to do together. You'll also receive deleted scenes from CLEARWATER and other treats, as well as be eligible for giveaways and other fabulousness as it arises.

You'll also be the first to know when COPPER: a Boldene Romance (Book 2) is available (summer of 2021—so keep reading for more about it).

The rest of the books in the BOLDENE series are in the works:

GOLD LEAF

HEAVY METAL

WILLOW

Most importantly, and you might know this or you might not, but here's the gist: we self-published authors thrive off of our reviews and the support of our devoted fans! I will always strive to deliver the best read I can for you, and I ask that if what I write resonates with you, please, please, please, leave me a review, I will be *forever* grateful.

Continue on to read more about COPPER: a Boldene Romance (Book 2)!

Esther Star reads and writes small town contemporary romance as a
required supplement for modern living; much like a multivitamin. She loves
sunshine, the smell of roses, frankincense, her kid, her man, and her cat.
She uses tarot, numerology, astrology, handwriting, and Dosha quizzes to
hack her life into near perfection and so do her characters. She believes
there is power in plant medicine and will sit still for anything about
ancient civilizations, spirituality, or modern science. She writes
emotionally intelligent characters who aim for honesty, with themselves
and each other, above all else.

Turn the page to read about COPPER: a Boldene Romance (Book 2).

COPPER: A BOLDENE ROMANCE
(BOOK 2)

AURORA COPPER KEEPS SVERE BENHAUS A SECRET.
She doesn't do high maintenance anything. She and Svere might both live in the same small town of Boldene and share the same circle of friends, but theirs in an undercover romance. Period. Aurora has enough responsibility with her ailing mother and fledgling career. But when her mother takes a turn for the worse, Aurora's priorities change, and she can no longer escape to work destination weddings and covert assignments.

Svere Benhaus has spent the last decade on the road, forging necessary relationships to grow his private investment firm. Focused on the prize, he rarely lingered with any of the exotic beauties used to sway his opinion on potential partnerships. But when he ran into hometown girl Aurora Copper in Amsterdam, and then again in Bali, Svere could not resist. He consented to her ridiculous terms and agreed to keep their escapades undercover whenever in Boldene.

And now that his best friend and Aurora's best friend are married, Svere and Aurora can't help but bump into each other. All the time. Much to Aurora's dismay, Svere is everywhere, pushing her to be open about everything including them and the gorgeous work hidden in her studio.

Bored chronicling the usual liminal moments of others, what will it take for Aurora to create some of her own?

COPPER is an emotionally intelligent small-town romance featuring a tight knit group of women who prefer to face life's lemons head on...but only after a shot of alcohol, a hit of pot, and a broad streak of sarcasm.

∾

Look for COPPER: a Boldene Romance (Book 2) in Esther Star's contemporary series, available summer of 2021. To be the first to know when it goes live, sign up for Esther's newsletter here: www.estherstar.com.

All the BOLDENE Romances:
    CLEARWATER
    COPPER
    GOLD LEAF
    HEAVY METAL
    WILLOW

Made in the USA
Las Vegas, NV
26 April 2021